PRETENSES

Steven didn't seem to be acting like himself at Cara's party. She watched anxiously as he left the table in the restaurant. "Jessica," she said, frowning, "has Steve been acting differently since he came home?"

"What do you mean?" Jessica asked.

"He seems distant. I'm going to go try to talk to him. I'll be back in a second," she said, pushing her chair back and standing. She found Steven sitting on a chair scanning a piece of pink stationery, his brow wrinkled.

"Hey," Cara said with a smile, coming up behind him and putting her hands on his shoulders, "what's that?"

Steven jumped. His face turned bright red, and he folded the stationery hastily. "Cara," he said, annoyed, "since when do you go sneaking up on people and read over their shoulders?"

Cara felt her face grow hot. "I wasn't sneaking!" she said indignantly. "I just came out here to make sure you were all right. Anyway, what difference would it make if I were looking over your shoulder? Since when do you get letters that you have to hide from me, y̲o̲u̲r̲ o̲w̲n̲ g̲i̲r̲l̲f̲r̲i̲e̲n̲d̲?"

"S̲_____ all," Steven said _____ ter into the brea_____ ed away.

Bantam Books in the Sweet Valley High Series
Ask your bookseller for the books you have missed

SWEET VALLEY HIGH

PRETENSES

Written by
Kate William

Created by
Francine Pascal

BANTAM BOOKS
TORONTO · NEW YORK · LONDON · SYDNEY · AUCKLAND

RL6, IL age 12 and up

PRETENSES
A Bantam Book / April 1988

Sweet Valley High is a trademark of Francine Pascal.

Conceived by Francine Pascal

Produced by Daniel Weiss Associates, Inc.
27 West 20th Street
New York, NY 10011

Cover art by James Mathewuse

ISBN 0-553-27064-8

Published simultaneously in the United States and Canada

PRINTED IN THE UNITED STATES OF AMERICA

O   0 9 8 7 6 5 4 3 2

PRETENSES

One

"I hate taking the bus to school," Jessica Wakefield grumbled to her friend Cara Walker. It was Wednesday morning, and the girls were taking the bus together to Sweet Valley High. Jessica's blue-green eyes flashed with impatience as she surveyed the crowded seats around them. If there was one thing Jessica didn't like, it was having to compromise, especially first thing in the morning! But her twin sister, Elizabeth, had taken the Fiat they shared to a doctor's appointment, leaving Jessica without a car. That meant taking the bus to Sweet Valley High with Cara—and several dozen others.

Cara giggled. "Come on, Jess. It's not so bad. You act like it's a fate worse than death to take the bus. I kind of like it." She grinned. "It gives

1

me time to reread the great letters your brother sends me, like the one I got this weekend. He's a terrific writer, Jess, and his letters are incredibly romantic." She pulled the letter out of her shoulder bag. "Just listen to this part," she began, her eyes shining with pleasure.

Jessica forgot how agonizing it was to take the bus as she regarded her friend. "Cara," she said seriously, "I've been meaning to talk to you about this. When are you two going to smarten up and drop this whole long-distance thing?" Cara had been dating Jessica's older brother, Steven, a college freshman at a nearby state university, for some time now. Although it had been her idea to fix them up in the first place, Jessica had recently decided that Cara and Steven were no longer an ideal couple. For one thing, she preferred having her friend all to herself, and for another, she was sick of so many of her good friends being involved in such serious relationships. Especially with Steven forty-five minutes away! What was the point? After all, there were plenty of good-looking guys right there in Sweet Valley. Lately it had been irritating her more than ever. And Cara—pretty, dark-haired Cara, who had always been so much fun—had really lost a lot of her spunk since she started going out with Steven. The old Cara was much wilder, much more fun. Now she was so—so *responsible*. Much more like Elizabeth than like Jessica!

"Don't start in on all that nonsense again," Cara warned her. "How many times have we been through this, Jess? You know I'm madly in love with Steve, so quit trying to talk me out of it. Besides," she added, smiling again, "we have more important things to talk about, like planning my birthday party. So you can just forget this nonsense. I *don't* need you to wreck my love life."

Although Cara's birthday was actually a few months earlier, both she and Steven had been going through a rough period at the time, so Cara hadn't really celebrated properly. She had recently decided to throw herself a belated party.

Jessica sighed and looked out the bus window at the beautiful southern California landscape. "OK," she said at last. But she couldn't help thinking that Cara was being awfully defensive about Steven. She had noticed recently how moody and preoccupied Cara seemed, and she was pretty certain something was wrong between the two of them. She was going to have to make a point of finding out exactly what was going on.

"I did something totally dumb," Cara confided as the bus lurched around a corner, getting nearer to the high school. "I mentioned to Abbie Richardson that I was having a party, and I think she thinks I'm going to invite her."

Jessica frowned. Abbie, a sweet-tempered brunette who had never spent much time with Jessica or any of her friends since ninth grade, suddenly seemed to be *everywhere*. "I don't know what the deal is with Abbie," Jessica complained. "Ever since she broke up with that guy from Palisades High, she's been hanging on everyone, trying to get herself invited to everything."

"I don't think that's what she's doing, Jessica," Cara said. "Actually, *I* was the one who brought it up. And she's really very nice. I'd like her to come. It's just that I'm having the party in a private room at the Marine House, and I can't afford to invite more than fourteen. I've gone over the guest list about a dozen times, and there's no one else I can possibly leave out."

"Don't worry," Jessica assured her. "I'm sure Abbie has forgotten all about it by now. Your party isn't for ages, anyway."

"It's a week from Sunday," Cara objected. "Not ages away!" Cara's voice was hesitant as

4

she said, "So you really don't think Abbie will mind if I don't invite her? It seems kind of rude after I brought it up."

Jessica made a face. "I wouldn't waste time thinking about it, Cara. Abbie Richardson managed to get along just fine without any of us for years. I'm sure she'll live if she misses this one little party."

"I guess you're right," Cara said reluctantly, even though she wasn't so sure. Just then the bus pulled into the parking lot, and total mayhem erupted as everyone tried to squeeze out of the narrow doors at once. In the crush, Cara forgot, for the moment, about Abbie Richardson.

Elizabeth Wakefield sighed and pushed her lunch tray away. "I don't understand it," she said to Penny Ayala, the editor of the student newspaper. "What do you suppose is wrong with *The Oracle*? Why isn't it as popular as it used to be?"

Elizabeth was completely devoted to the school paper. She hoped to be a writer one day, and she wanted all the experience in journalism she could get. Jessica was constantly teasing her about staying locked inside the *Oracle* office on gorgeous sunny afternoons, afternoons when Jessica was invariably at the beach or at least outside for cheerleading practice. But working on the newspaper didn't seem like a sacrifice to Elizabeth. And, as she often reminded her twin sister, she had gotten to know her boyfriend, Jeffrey French, at the newspaper office. So it wasn't all work and no play after all!

Jeffrey, who had moved to Sweet Valley from Oregon in the middle of the junior year, was a photographer for the paper. Now he put his hand over Elizabeth's and patted it affectionately. Penny, Elizabeth, and Jeffrey had met at lunch to discuss the questionnaire *The Oracle* had distributed to the student body the week before. It seemed that Sweet Valley High wasn't quite as interested in its school paper as it had been the past few years.

"Maybe my column hasn't been exciting enough," Elizabeth said. Her job was to write the "Eyes and Ears" column, a weekly gossip feature that kept everyone aware of who had been seen where with whom. It had always been one of the most popular features in *The Oracle*.

Winston Egbert, a lanky junior who was widely acknowledged as the class clown, set his tray down next to Penny's. "Any room here?

6

Hey," he added, "why all the long faces? You guys look like you just won second prize in the Sweet Valley High sweepstakes."

When no one responded, Winston looked pained. "Aren't you even going to ask what second prize is?" he demanded.

"OK," Jeffrey said. "What's second prize in the Sweet Valley High sweepstakes?"

"Two lunches," Winston said cheerfully, bowing as everyone burst out laughing.

"We're talking about the questionnaire *The Oracle* sent out last week," Penny told him. "We're all worried because the responses showed that people are less enthusiastic about the paper than they were the last time we took a poll. We're trying to figure out what we can do to make the paper more lively."

"Simple," Winston said, unwrapping an ice-cream sandwich with great attention.

Elizabeth glanced at Jeffrey. "Simple?" she repeated to Winston. "You mean you know what's missing?"

"Of course," Winston said with authority. "It should be obvious. Look, you've got a great photographer, right?" He patted Jeffrey on the shoulder. "You've got a great editor and some of the best writers around. What you don't

7

have"—he took a bite of ice cream—"is humor. No cartoons. No comic strip. No puzzles. Nothing funny in the whole darn paper."

"He's right," Penny said to Elizabeth. "I never even thought of that. Did you?"

Elizabeth had to admit she hadn't. "Winston, that's a great idea! If we add a humorous feature to the paper, I bet people will like it every bit as much as they did when we first started putting the paper out!"

"The question is, what kind of funny feature?" Jeffrey said musingly. All eyes fell on Winston, who pretended to writhe with pain.

"Quit looking at me," he said with a groan, covering his face with his hands. "I can't stand it."

"Winston," Penny said pleadingly, "how would you like to be the new humor editor? Just come up with something truly hilarious by next week and make everyone say how much they love the paper again."

"Not me," Winston said. "I happen to have an incredibly demanding schedule. David Letterman and Johnny Carson have both been clamoring for my jokes."

"Winston!" Elizabeth shrieked. "We need you. Can't you see how badly *The Oracle* needs a good shot of humor?"

"Of course I can. I'm the one who suggested it," Winston said calmly. "But listen, seriously, guys, I couldn't possibly accept the job. I promised my parents I'd get my grades up by next marking period, and if I don't, I have a feeling they're going to keep me from ever telling a joke again. So no more extracurricular stuff till my grades are as good as Elizabeth Wakefield's." He winked at Elizabeth. "Don't look so depressed," he added, patting her on the arm. "Why don't you guys just handle this the good old American way? Run a competition!"

"That's not a bad idea," Penny said thoughtfully. "What do you think, guys? Maybe we could put Olivia in charge of it." Olivia Davidson was the arts editor of the paper.

"I think it's a great idea," Winston said vehemently. "In fact, I'm even willing to work as a consultant—for a nominal fee, of course." Everyone laughed, and he pretended to look hurt. "Nobody knows how tough it is having a good sense of humor. It's so hard to get taken seriously!"

Penny and Elizabeth immediately began to discuss plans for the humor competition. Jeffrey joined in, and before long they had the plans firmed up. They decided to advertise the competition that very afternoon. Entries would be due a week from Thursday. All they had to do now was present the idea to Mr. Collins, the popular English teacher who also served as adviser to the *The Oracle*. He was almost certain to approve of whatever they chose to do.

The four of them were so involved in their conversation that they didn't even notice when Abbie Richardson approached their table, balancing her tray awkwardly in her small hands. "Hey," she said in a soft voice, "mind if I join you?"

"Not at all," Elizabeth said at once, sliding over to make room for the pretty girl. She gave Abbie a welcoming smile, trying to hide the surprise she felt that Abbie had come over to sit with them. She barely knew Abbie. Maybe Winston did, or Penny. But the others seemed as surprised as Elizabeth, and the conversation faltered a little.

Abbie Richardson had been friendly with Jessica in ninth grade. In fact, for a few months they had been practically inseparable. Then Abbie had dropped out of the picture. Elizabeth hadn't really kept up with all the details, but as far as she could remember, Abbie had met a tenth-grader from Palisades High—Doug Brewster, a baseball player. From then on Abbie spent all her free time with Doug and his friends. She sat on the Palisades' side when the two schools played each other and never bothered to keep up her friendships with people from Sweet Valley High. That was two whole years ago, and since then most people had forgotten all about Abbie Richardson, at least, until a few weeks ago when Abbie and Doug broke up. Shortly after the breakup, Abbie started showing up in places where she hadn't been seen for ages.

Although Elizabeth knew little about Abbie, she liked her. There was something sweet and appealing in her expression. She was strikingly pretty in a demure way, her dark brown hair as fine as satin and her eyes a clear light blue. Everything about her was delicate—her ivory complexion, her dainty hands, her soft smile. Even her voice was sweet and well modulated.

"We're just talking about running a competition for a new humor feature in *The Oracle*," Penny said to Abbie and went on to explain the idea the group had come up with.

Abbie's eyes lit up. "I love *The Oracle*," she said quickly. "Is there anything I can do to help?"

Elizabeth was surprised. It wasn't exactly typ-

11

ical to hear someone volunteer, especially someone with no connection to the paper.

Penny smiled. "Maybe you can. We're going to need to make posters to advertise the contest. If you really want to, Abbie . . ."

"Oh, I'd love to!" Abbie said quickly. She blushed slightly under Winston's scrutinizing gaze.

"You know, Abbie is an ace cartoonist," Winston said thoughtfully. "Shouldn't you be trying out yourself instead of making the posters?" he asked Abbie. He turned to the others to explain that he and Abbie had been in an art class together the year before, and she had been one of the most talented students in the class.

Abbie shrugged. "I think I'd rather help Penny and Liz make posters," she said matter-of-factly. "Anyway, Winston is exaggerating."

Elizabeth looked at her with increasing interest. Abbie didn't seem the sort of girl to put herself down. Winston wouldn't have said she was talented if she wasn't. So why would she rather help make posters than enter the competition? It didn't make sense.

"I'd better take my tray up," Penny said, brushing the crumbs from her lap. "I've got to go talk to Mr. Collins about our new scheme."

"Let me take it for you," Abbie said, jumping

12

to her feet and taking the tray before Penny could say a word in protest.

Penny stared at her. "Uh, thanks," she said, confused.

"What a nice girl," Jeffrey said, watching Abbie hurry off with Penny's tray.

Elizabeth and Penny exchanged glances. Elizabeth wondered if Penny was thinking the same thing she was. *Nice* wasn't the word. Abbie seemed too good to be true!

Two

"Anyone home?" Elizabeth called later that afternoon as she opened the front door to the Wakefields' comfortable split-level house.

"We're in here," Jessica called from the living room, where she and Cara had spread their homework all over the carpet only to ignore it. They were watching Jessica's favorite soap opera on TV.

Elizabeth laughed when she walked into the room. "Hard at work, as usual," she said dryly. Homework was the bane of her twin sister's existence. Luckily there were distractions such as radio and television to help her get through the ordeal!

"You two crack me up," Cara said, pushing a strand of hair away from her face. "How is it possible to look like clones and act like total opposites?"

Elizabeth and Jessica grinned at each other. They had asked themselves the same question for so long now, it was hard to believe they hadn't figured out a sensible answer. Cara was right. On the outside they were mirror images— sun-streaked blond hair, blue-green eyes the color of the Pacific, tiny dimples that showed when they smiled, and shapely size-six figures. Their voices were identical, and their gestures were the same. It was no wonder people had a hard time telling them apart!

But that was it as far as identical went. Elizabeth couldn't believe that she was only four minutes older than her twin. Sometimes those minutes felt like years! Not that Jessica was immature. She could act much older than sixteen—especially if a cute older guy was around to watch her. It was just that Jessica thrived on excitement and change. Whatever the latest fad, Jessica had to be in on it. She wore the newest fashions, which she got sick of almost as soon as the bills were paid, if not sooner. She went through hobbies with feverish zeal and got bored easily, so easily that she complained that her twin sister was set a whole gear too slow. "That's why I don't wear a watch," Jessica was fond of saying. "Because I like to go at *my* own pace." Elizabeth always rolled her eyes at this remark. It was so typical of Jessica—trying to make a virtue out of an honest-to-goodness bad habit! She was notoriously late to everything. She couldn't be counted on for anything but excitement—and trouble. More times than she could count, Elizabeth had been called on to bail her sister out of difficult situations. And sometimes Jessica's antics got to be more than she could bear. But deep down the twins loved each other with all their hearts, and Elizabeth could never stay mad at Jessica for very long.

Elizabeth, in contrast to her impulsive twin, possessed a calm, even-tempered personality. She was as fair and judicious as her sister was hot-tempered and irrational. Sometimes Elizabeth thought it was her desire to be a journalist that made her so objective. Whatever the cause, she prided herself on looking before she leaped whereas Jessica *never* looked.

The twins had few friends in common, though they often did things together. Jessica preferred the company of people such as Cara, Lila Fowler, and Amy Sutton—popular, stylish girls who were active members of Pi Beta Alpha, the exclusive sorority of which Jessica was the president. She also numbered some good friends among the cheerleading squad, which she co-captained. Elizabeth's friends struck Jessica as boring. Enid Rollins, for instance, Elizabeth's best friend and one of the nicest, most dependable girls at school as far as Elizabeth was concerned, seemed to Jessica to be the next dullest thing after homework. Jessica liked Jeffrey French, her twin's boyfriend, but lately she was on a campaign against serious relationships and was trying her hardest to get Elizabeth—like Cara—to consider playing the field.

"We have our differences," Elizabeth said now, giving Cara a mild smile. "But we manage to get along, for limited periods of time, anyway." The three of them decided to have something to eat, and as they sat at the kitchen table, Elizabeth began to fill Jessica and Cara in on Winston's idea for *The Oracle*. Both girls thought a comedy feature was a great idea.

They were all batting ideas around when the telephone rang. Jessica lunged for the wall phone, almost knocking her twin over. "Oh, hi," she said, sounding disappointed. "It's Steven," she announced, shaking her head at the look of delight that came over Cara's face. "This long-distance stuff," she muttered. "Steve, when are you coming home to visit? Cara looks like she's pining away."

"That's why I'm calling," Steven said. He sounded to Jessica as if he had a cold. "A doctor at the health service here thinks I may have allergies or a sinus problem. He wants me to come home for some pretty intense tests. I'll be bringing lots of classwork with me because I have to see a couple of doctors and have all kinds of tests, including sinus X rays and stuff like that. So it might take awhile. Anyway, I'm feeling so lousy, I'm kind of looking forward to being home and doing my work there."

Jessica giggled. "Maybe you're allergic to college. You come home often enough."

Cara's face looked even brighter. "Is he coming home? Let me talk to him," she begged, snatching the telephone out of Jessica's hand.

Jessica frowned at her friend the whole time Cara spoke. She listened intently as Cara went on and on about how great it would be to have Steven around, especially with her party coming up. Whatever problems Jessica had thought she had noticed between Cara and Steven before seemed to have disappeared. When Cara hung up, Jessica gave her a long look.

"You'd better watch it, Cara. You know the old saying about familiarity breeding contempt. If Steven's going to be around here for almost two weeks, you might start getting on each other's nerves. What you two need is a little mystery in your relationship."

Cara looked surprised. "What do you mean? Has Steve been saying something to you about us? Do you think he's getting sick of me?"

"Don't get paranoid," Jessica advised. "That's the last thing you need. It's just that I happen to have been reading a great article in *Ingenue* magazine about this. If you don't keep men guessing a little, all the spark goes out of the relationship. If I were you, I'd be a little—you know—*aloof*. Do something to surprise him, make things more romantic between you. It's important not to let him start taking you for granted."

Cara looked slightly confused. "But things have been fine between us lately, Jess. Maybe there isn't much mystery in our relationship, but there isn't any miscommunication either. We always know just where we stand with each other. We're very open about things. Isn't that the way it should be?"

Jessica shrugged. "Open is fine, if you want someone to take you for granted. My own feeling is that girls should be a little less open and a lot more mysterious. Kind of the way it used to be in the movies. I mean, look at Lania Louise, for instance." Lania was Jessica's favorite soap opera character that week. "You never see Lania being *open* with any of the men she loves, do you?"

"You've got a point," Cara said, looking worried.

Elizabeth laughed. "Right, Jess. I'm surprised at you. If you're such an expert on romance, why aren't you going out with anyone right now?"

Jessica made a face. "Because I'd rather not be involved with just one guy, thank you. I'm sick of all the guys at school anyway."

Elizabeth got to her feet. "Well, it sounds to me as though Steve's going to need sympathy and support. Being sick can't be any fun. Who needs mystery when your nose is running, your eyes are itching, and you can't stop sneezing?"

Cara didn't answer, but Jessica said, "I think you're wrong, Liz. Steve needs something to take his mind off his problems." She was glad she had said something. After all, Cara was one of her best friends and Steven was her brother. If she couldn't convince them that they'd be better off not being so serious, then the least she could do was to keep them from getting into a real rut.

*   *   *

21

"Hi, sweetheart," Mrs. Richardson said when Abbie wandered into the kitchen after school, her arms filled with books. "How was your day?"

Abbie thought first before answering. Much as she adored her mother, lately Abbie felt her mother was getting too involved in her activities. Ever since Abbie had broken up with Doug, it seemed that telling her mother the simplest thing often led to long, drawn-out discussions. Her mother was a psychologist, and Abbie knew she couldn't help letting her professional side show when she talked with Abbie about her social life.

"It was fine, Mom," she said in a neutral voice, helping herself to an apple from the refrigerator. "Actually, it was a pretty good day." She told her mother about sitting with Winston, Elizabeth, Penny, and Jeffrey at lunch and volunteering to help advertise the competition for the paper.

"That's wonderful, honey. Are you going to submit some cartoons for the competition? I'm sure they'd be a real hit," Mrs. Richardson said warmly.

"I'm considering it," Abbie admitted, taking a bite out of the apple. "Elizabeth Wakefield is so nice, Mom, I really want to get to know her better." She paused to chew and then went on. "I hope I can get to be friends with her." She was thinking that submitting cartoons for the paper's competition might be the best way. Abbie had been noticing Elizabeth from afar for a while now, and she secretly thought Elizabeth was one of the smartest, nicest girls at school. Now that Abbie was no longer spending time with the kids from Palisades High, she was anxious to start making some new friends. And if there was one person Abbie wanted for a friend, it was Elizabeth!

"Honey, I'm delighted," her mother said sincerely. "It sounds like you're really going after what *you* want." She frowned. "When you were with Doug, you seemed to spend all your time accommodating him. You saw *his* friends, not yours. You were the one who was forever doing things to help him, not the other way around. It's just wonderful to see you making new friends and starting to have a life of your own."

Abbie didn't answer. Sometimes she thought her mother was a little too critical of Doug, but in this case she had to admit she had a point. Their relationship hadn't been very equal. Doug was a year older than Abbie, and from the start she had felt compelled to try to impress him, to do whatever she could to make him happy.

Unfortunately, it hadn't gone the other way. Doug hadn't given as much love back as he'd taken. When they decided to split up, Abbie was the one who suffered most. Doug still had his friends, his sports, his familiar, comfortable life. Abbie was the one who had given up everything for Doug. Now, with Doug gone, she had to learn to start doing things for herself. She wasn't finding it easy, but she felt hopeful she would make more friends in time.

"You know what else, Mom? A few days ago Cara Walker told me about the fancy party she's having next weekend, and I'm sure she's going to invite me. I think it's going to be really fun. It's at the Marine House, right on the water. What do you think I should wear?"

Mrs. Richardson beamed at her daughter. "Oh, honey, we should buy you a new dress. The Marine House is supposed to be gorgeous. Why don't we go shopping tonight after dinner?" She gave Abbie a spontaneous hug. "I'm so happy for you, dear. Your social life is really taking off!"

Abbie blushed with pleasure. Her mother was as happy as she was about the invitation. That was the positive side of having a mother who cared so much about what she did!

"You know," Abbie said with sudden determination, "I think I *am* going to submit a cartoon strip to *The Oracle*. I'm going to go upstairs and see what kind of ideas I can come up with."

Abbie worked on her cartoon strip until dinner. She tried a couple of different ideas—one about animals, one about creatures from outer space—before deciding to set her cartoon strip closer to home. She called the strip "Jenny," and the main character, Jenny Bain, was a sixteen-year-old high school student just like Abbie. In fact, Abbie's middle name was Bain, an old family name, which made the identification even stronger. Abbie decided the cartoon would be about the life of an average girl in high school who went through the same ups and downs that most teenagers did. The first strip was about breaking up with a boyfriend. In the first panel Jenny was talking to her mother, complaining. "When I was going out with John, I felt terrible about myself. All I could do was sit around and worry about him. We stopped having fun, and I felt like it was all my fault."

"So, how do you feel now?" Jenny's mother asked in the second panel.

"Well, everything's different now. John and I

have split up, and I don't have anyone to blame but myself for anything that happens."

"Well, it's Friday night, sweetheart. What are you going to do? Are you going to see some friends? Go to a movie?"

"Nah," Jenny said in the last panel. "I think I'll just sit around and worry for a while about what I did to make things fall apart!"

Abbie liked the cartoon a lot. She was sure she wouldn't be the only one able to identify with Jenny.

In fact, she liked the cartoon strip so much, she decided she would definitely submit it to *The Oracle* for the competition. She just hoped Elizabeth liked it. As far as Abbie was concerned these days, Elizabeth Wakefield could do no wrong. If she liked the cartoon, Abbie would believe it was good.

Three

The twins had decided to prepare a special dinner for Steven's homecoming Friday evening. "We have to do something to make him feel better," Elizabeth had said.

Jessica was outside on the patio, grilling hamburgers, while Elizabeth sat at the outdoor table, chopping vegetables for a big tossed salad. They had also decided to roast corn on the grill.

"Mom and Dad should be home soon," Jessica said. Their mother, an interior designer, and their father, an attorney, had both promised to get home early that night. Elizabeth didn't answer, but Jessica continued talking. "I hope Steven isn't allergic to hamburgers," she called to Elizabeth from her perch at the barbecue.

Elizabeth was clearly thinking about something else while she prepared the salad. "Hey," she said reflectively, "we had a meeting about the new feature in *The Oracle* this afternoon. A lot of people showed up with good ideas. Abbie is talking about drawing a cartoon strip that sounds great. And you'll never guess who else showed up, Jess. Amy Sutton. Can you believe it? She had the idea of writing a kind of mock Miss Manners column." Amy Sutton was a close friend of Jessica's. Elizabeth, who had been friendly with Amy years ago, thought she had become cliquish and boy-crazy. "The strangest thing of all is that Abbie started offering to help Amy with her proposal. Since it looks like Amy's her strongest competition, I couldn't help thinking that was a little weird."

"What is it about Abbie Richardson? All of a sudden she seems to be running for Miss Congeniality or something. She's acting like everyone's best friend. Just a few months ago no one ever saw her."

"Well, try to be sympathetic, Jess," Elizabeth said as she seasoned the salad. "Until she broke up with Doug, she was understandably less interested in getting to know people at school. Now I think she's trying hard to make friends. Frankly, I don't see anything wrong with it. She's a really nice girl. It's not like she's got some kind of sneaky motive or anything. All she wants is to be friendly."

Jessica wrinkled her nose. "It gets on my nerves when people are that nice. I'm always sure they want something."

Elizabeth couldn't resist a laugh at this point. "I wonder why," she said sardonically. "Jessica, has it ever occurred to you that the rest of the world doesn't operate by Jessica Wakefield's standards?"

Jessica shrugged. "Well, all I know is that she bothers me. She's too . . . I don't know, too *nice*. You should've seen her today in art class. She actually volunteered to clean up after everyone! Not that I wasn't glad at the time, since I was wearing my new white cotton knit shirt. I mean, the last thing I wanted was to get oil paint all over it. But it still seemed weird. I told Cara, and she thought it was weird, too."

"Speaking of Cara," Elizabeth said, "is she coming over tonight to see Steven?" She was actually glad to have an excuse to change the subject. She felt slightly uncomfortable talking about Abbie, although she wasn't sure why. Maybe it was because she didn't really know her that well yet, and she hated to make judgments prematurely.

Jessica nodded. "She's been going on and on

all day about seeing Steve. God, you'd think it had been two months since they'd seen each other, not two weeks!"

Elizabeth smiled. She could imagine two weeks feeling like an eternity if she and Jeffrey were separated for that long.

"Hellooo, anyone home?" a familiar voice called.

"Steve!" the twins cried in unison. The next minute they were engulfing their older brother in twin hugs.

"Whoa!" He laughed, then stepped back and grinned at them. "I'm sickly, remember? The doctor told me there's a distinct chance I could be allergic to twins. Especially blond twins."

"You don't look sick," Jessica argued, putting her head to one side and studying her brother. In fact, Steven looked as handsome as ever, just like a younger version of their father, with his dark hair, broad shoulders, and eyes that crinkled at the corners when he smiled.

"I'm not really sick. I just can't breathe too well," Steven said, setting his bags down in the front hall. "Are Mom and Dad still at work?" When both girls nodded, he said, "Good, quick, fill me in on all the gossip before they get here."

Elizabeth winked at her sister. She loved having her brother at home; their family was complete again.

　　　　*　　　*　　　*

"I can't believe how much I missed you," Cara told Steven later that night. They were sitting out by the Wakefields' pool, and Cara couldn't help thinking how romantic the setting was. The moonlight was reflected on the water, and the air was the perfect temperature, slightly balmy and scented with flowers.

Steven sneezed. "You know," he said, taking out a tissue, "we might be better off inside. This pollen—"

Cara couldn't help noticing that Steven had dropped her hand in an effort to get the tissue. He didn't bother to reach for it again, either. *Remember what Jessica said*, a little voice reminded her. Was Steven really getting tired of her? He hadn't seemed all that excited to see her when she arrived at the Wakefields' that evening, and he hadn't paid much attention to her since then.

"Fine," she said in a short, curt tone. "We can go back inside if you want." *But your family is in the living room, and we won't be alone*, she thought to herself. She gave Steven a significant look, which meant, loud and clear, "I'd rather stay out here alone with you and be romantic."

But if Steven noticed, he misread her meaning. "Phew," he said, getting to his feet. "I'm

31

glad you don't mind, Cara. I think something out here is really making me feel worse."

Cara didn't say a word. Instead she followed Steven inside and tried to hide her impatience as they sat down with the rest of the Wakefields. When Steven excused himself to go upstairs and take some medicine, Jessica leaned over to whisper conspiratorially in Cara's ear. "Not much of a romantic reunion, huh?" she said. "See what I mean? You two need mystery, Cara. Mystery."

By the end of the evening, Cara was beginning to think Jessica might be right. It wasn't just that Steven wasn't being romantic. That made sense, and she couldn't really blame him. After all, the poor guy was clearly miserable. His nose was running, and his eyes were puffy and watery.

But even so, he could have carried on a conversation with her, Cara thought. He had barely said a word to her all night. He really seemed to be thinking about something else.

"Let's take a walk," she said finally, unable to bear it any longer. She hadn't seen him in weeks—*weeks*—and he was treating her like she was his kid sister!

"OK," Steven said, not looking thrilled.

"Is anything wrong? You seem preoccupied,"

Cara observed as they strolled out onto the sidewalk.

"I'm a little worried about a paper I'm working on for my history class. In fact, this was a terrible time of the term for me to get sick. I've got tons of stuff to do, and you know how badly I want to get good grades this semester." He didn't notice the disappointed expression on Cara's face.

"Hey," she said softly, slipping her arm through his, "I missed you. I'm glad you're back."

Steven looked down at her with surprise. For a moment she thought she saw an expression of annoyance in his dark eyes. "Cara, I don't feel very well. It's not like this is a vacation. Unless I can get a lot of stuff done while I'm at home . . ."

Cara pulled her arm back abruptly. "I'm sorry," she said quickly. "I only meant that it's nice to see you, that's all."

Steven's eyes softened. "I'm sorry," he said, pulling her close to him. "You'll have to bear with me, Cara. I just feel rotten. And the pills the doctor at school gave me are making me tired and cranky. I'm glad to see you, too. And I've missed you."

Cara still felt uneasy. Steven didn't sound

like himself. Was it really because he was sick, or was it something else? Again she thought that perhaps Jessica was right. Perhaps their relationship *was* beginning to get humdrum. It sure didn't seem that there were any fireworks right now. She wondered if there *was* some way to get some mystery back in their relationship.

"OK, Cara, tell us more about your party," Lila Fowler said. It was lunchtime on the Thursday before the party, and Jessica, Cara, and Lila had gathered with a group of their friends at a corner table. Amy Sutton, Jean West, Sandra Bacon, and Maria Santelli, friends of Jessica's from the cheerleading squad, were all there.

"It's Sunday at one o'clock, right?" Maria asked.

Cara nodded glumly. She hadn't eaten much of her lunch. She actually wasn't feeling that hungry. *Whatever Steven has must be infectious*, she thought with a sigh. She hadn't been feeling well since he'd come home.

Soon an animated discussion of Cara's party was taking place. Lila Fowler, the richest girl in school and someone who never lost an opportunity to remind people of it, declared that the Marine House was just like a little place in Paris she had been to with her father. Amy Sutton wanted to know who was invited. Jessica got into an argument with everyone else about whether to wear dresses or pants. The conversation was so lively that no one noticed Abbie Richardson until she was almost at the table.

"Shhh," Cara said, her facing turning red.

"Can I sit with you guys, or are you talking about something private?" Abbie asked.

"We're only talking about—"

"Sure!" Cara said loudly, kicking Jessica under the table. "We were talking about the competition for a humor feature in *The Oracle*. We all think it's a great idea, just what the paper needs to liven it up."

Feeling shy, Abbie set her tray down. She had a feeling that wasn't what they had been talking about at all. She looked at Cara out of the corner of her eye as she began to eat her lunch. When was Cara going to tell her more about her birthday party? Abbie had been waiting every day to get an invitation in the mail or hear from Cara on the phone. Actually, she felt kind of awkward about it, and she had come over to join Cara and her friends with the hope that Cara would straighten everything out.

Cara wouldn't have told her about the party

if she wasn't going to invite her, would she? But then why hadn't she said anything yet?

Abbie waited patiently for the conversation to turn to Cara's party, but the group seemed to be studiously avoiding the topic. Abbie eyed the others with curiosity as she ate her chicken salad. Suddenly an explanation crossed her mind. Maybe Cara hadn't invited some of these girls. After all, the Marine House had to be an expensive place; Cara wouldn't be able to invite a lot of people. Maybe Jean hadn't been included, or Sandra. Cara would be too polite to bring it up in front of them if they hadn't been invited.

This made Abbie feel better, and by the time lunch was over, she was certain that she had hit on the reason for Cara's silence. No doubt Cara would call her that very evening and tell her to be tactful about the luncheon for Jean's or Sandra's sake.

Cara started to complain about a homework assignment in math, and Abbie couldn't resist offering to help her out. "I've got a study hall this afternoon. If you're free, I could go over the problems with you," she said.

Cara looked slightly embarrassed. "Oh, that's OK, Abbie. Thanks for offering, but I can probably figure them out if I plug away for a while."

"Please let me help," Abbie said. "I'd really

like to." She didn't understand why Cara looked so reluctant. Didn't she realize how much Abbie liked helping people?

"Hey, Abbie!" Elizabeth shouted, hurrying down the hallway. "Guess what! You and Amy Sutton are the two finalists in the competition. We didn't realize so many people would enter, and you two tied. Mr. Collins wants each of you to submit another entry. He said that whoever wins is going to have to do a column or cartoon every week, and he wants to make sure that that person can keep up the pace. He'll make the final decision. Isn't it great that you're a finalist?"

Abbie's eyes lit up. "Oh, Liz, I'm so happy." She felt shy all of a sudden. "You really think the cartoon is OK?"

"OK?" Elizabeth echoed incredulously. "I think it's fabulous." She started telling Abbie all the wonderful things everyone had said about her work as a cartoonist, everyone from Winston to Mr. Collins. Abbie looked pleased, if unconvinced.

"I think my old boyfriend gave me a hang-up about my art," Abbie said with a sigh when Elizabeth was through. "Doug was always saying that cartoons are second-rate—not real art. His mother is a painter, and he looks up to her a lot. He doesn't think it takes much talent to do cartoons well."

"He doesn't sound worthy of you," Elizabeth said firmly. "If that's the way he felt, I'm glad you two broke up." She patted Abbie on the shoulder. "Anyway, I'm glad I get to be the one to tell you. Of course, it's not over yet. You'll have to submit another strip by next Thursday."

Abbie nodded. The only event on her calendar was Cara's party, so she would have plenty of time, Abbie thought. She had a sudden urge to ask Elizabeth about the party. Elizabeth would know the best way to approach Cara.

But Abbie didn't want to burden Elizabeth with her problems. That wasn't the way to make friends, she reminded herself. The way to make friends was to be nice to people, to listen to them, to offer to help them, not to dump your own troubles on their shoulders.

Abbie thanked Elizabeth warmly for all her help and sighed as she watched her walk down the hallway. She wished she were Elizabeth Wakefield—she was so popular, so self-assured.

But wishing wasn't going to get her anywhere. Abbie sighed again. She still felt lonesome every afternoon. This was the time that, in the old days, Doug would have been waiting for her outside in his Jeep. They would have driven over to his house, met some of his friends, spent the entire afternoon together. Abbie knew she was better off without Doug, but she couldn't help missing him. The afternoons felt pretty empty without him.

Still, she reminded herself, she had gotten a lot of encouragement about her cartoon strip, and now she was a finalist in the competition. Imagine if "Jenny" were picked and ran each week in *The Oracle*. That would really be something. Then she would have something important to do with her free time. Besides, right now she had Cara's party to look forward to. She was finally making some friends of her own, making a life for herself without Doug.

And just to remind herself of that, Abbie was going to stop at the mall on the way home and buy a birthday present for Cara.

Four

By Sunday morning Abbie couldn't kid herself anymore about Cara's birthday party. There was no way Cara was going to include her, she thought. Why had she ever mentioned it? Was she just trying to torment her?

"Abbie?" Mrs. Richardson knocked gently on her daughter's bedroom door. "Honey, what's wrong? Why are you in bed? I thought today was Cara Walker's birthday lunch."

Abbie pulled the sheet farther up over her face, avoiding her mother's gaze as she poked her head in to look at her. "I don't feel well," she said, hoping she sounded convincing. "Mom, I don't think I'm going to be able to go to Cara's party. I've got a terrible sore throat, and my head is killing me." Her eyes filled with tears—

41

genuine tears—and she bit her lip to keep from crying. She felt so humiliated. She thought of the new dress her mother had bought her, and the silver ring she'd chosen for Cara at the mall. If only she had never told her mother about the party! The disappointed look on her mother's face was almost more than she could bear.

"Sweetheart, what a shame," Mrs. Richardson said, coming over and putting her hand on Abbie's forehead. "I know how much you were looking forward to it." She frowned. "You don't feel warm. How long has your throat been hurting? Maybe we should call Dr. Griffin."

Abbie tossed fretfully. "No, Mom, don't call the doctor. I'm sure I'm just getting the flu. Lots of kids at school have been sick." She tried to squirm out from under her mother's penetrating gaze. If her parents found out the truth, Abbie knew she would die. *God, what a reject I am*, she thought. *Here I go on and on and on about this party, and Cara ends up not even inviting me.*

"You sure you don't feel up to going?" Mrs. Richardson asked, smoothing the hair off Abbie's forehead. "Maybe if you took a couple of aspirin and had some tea, I could drive you straight to the Marine House."

Ha! Abbie thought bitterly. That would really surprise everyone, especially Cara. "No, Mom," she managed, her voice faltering a little. "I really feel lousy. I'm just going to stay in bed."

It was true. She really did feel terrible, but not because her throat hurt. Abbie's ego was the thing that was hurting, and all the aspirin in the world wasn't going to make that go away.

Ever since Thursday's lunch, when she had been convinced Cara was going to let her know soon about the party, she had been more and more anxious about the whole thing. She kept waiting for Cara to say something to her or call her up. Finally on Friday afternoon Abbie couldn't stand it anymore, so she invented an excuse to call Cara. She claimed she needed some history notes. She could tell Cara knew that wasn't why she called, but if Cara suspected the real reason, she didn't make it any easier for Abbie. The conversation was stilted, and nothing was said about Cara's birthday. That was the final straw. Abbie knew then that she had been left out.

What she couldn't figure out was *why*. Abbie didn't know Cara that well, but she had always liked her. They'd been in the same history class for two years now and occasionally helped each other out with homework, that sort of thing. Several times they had had lunch together. Abbie had never done anything to hurt Cara, and she couldn't think of a single reason why Cara would want to hurt her.

Suddenly a thought struck her. Perhaps Elizabeth would know why Cara had changed her mind about inviting her. It was twelve o'clock. The party wasn't supposed to start until one or one-thirty. If she'd done something to insult Cara, maybe Elizabeth would know about it and there would be time to straighten things out before the party got under way. Abbie knew her plan was desperate, but she didn't care. Jumping out of bed, she hurried over to her desk and dialed the Wakefields' number.

"Abbie!" Elizabeth said, sounding surprised. "How are you? Listen, I can't talk right now. I'm actually just on my way out the door."

Abbie bit her lip. "You're going to Cara's party, aren't you?" she said, trying to sound cheerful.

"Yes," Elizabeth said, sounding surprised. "Can I call you back later? I should be home in a few hours."

Abbie stared at the receiver in her hand. What a stupid idea this had been. How would Elizabeth know why Cara had mentioned the party to her and then never said another word? Abbie felt silly and embarrassed. "Fine, call me later. I just wanted to ask you something about the 'Jenny' cartoon."

"Listen, Abbie, I've been meaning to ask you to come over anyway. Why don't you plan on coming home with me tomorrow after school? We can sit down and brainstorm about the cartoon together. Would that be OK with you?"

Abbie twisted the telephone cord. "That would be nice," she said. "Thanks, Liz."

"Good. I'll see you in school tomorrow, then," Elizabeth said.

"Oh, and have fun at Cara's," Abbie added. She felt a distinct pang. The thought of all of them sitting down to a great lunch at the Marine House made her eyes fill with tears. What had she done to hurt Cara? Why hadn't Cara at least called and explained why she had changed her mind? "Liz," she blurted suddenly, "did Cara ever tell you why she didn't end up inviting me to the party? She mentioned it to me a while ago but then never said another word about it."

Elizabeth sounded really embarrassed now. "You're kidding," she said. "Abbie, that's awful. That doesn't sound at all like Cara! But, no, she never said a word to me about it."

"Oh," Abbie said in a small voice. "Well, I just thought I'd see if you knew."

"I've got to go," Elizabeth said, sounding upset. "But if there's some way I can ask Cara about it, I will."

"Don't bother," Abbie said quickly. "It was obviously just a misunderstanding." She could tell how uncomfortable Elizabeth felt, and she was instantly sorry that she had burdened her. Another mistake, she thought, hating herself as she hung up the phone.

Abbie sighed as she sat forlornly at her desk. One thing was clear: She had obviously been going about things the wrong way. Making friends just wasn't as easy now as it had been when she was younger. Well, she was just going to have to bend over backward to do nice things for people to get them to like her. Maybe there were some things she could do to help Elizabeth in exchange for her advice about the "Jenny" strip.

Frowning, she picked up the silver ring she had chosen for Cara. Maybe Elizabeth would like it. Why not? It was only a small token, but it was a tiny way of showing Elizabeth how grateful she was for her friendship and advice.

Jessica was even more impressed by the Marine House than she had expected to be. The glamorous restaurant was set right on the water, and the room Cara had reserved for her party overlooked the boats in the harbor. The table was covered with snowy white linen, and there were two floral arrangements on it. The whole place looked like a movie set. Cara sat at the head of the table, with Steven at her right side and Jessica at her left. Elizabeth and Jeffrey were down at the far end with Lila, Sandra, Manuel Lopez—Sandra's boyfriend—and Jean and her boyfriend, Tom McKay. Winston Egbert, looking subdued and solemn in navy jacket and tie, sat toward the center of the table. Across from Winston was Maria Santelli, his girlfriend, who was on the cheerleading squad with Jessica, Sandra, and Jean. Amy Sutton was next to Winston, and across from her was Bruce Patman, a senior—and the richest guy at school.

Amy and Bruce had a troubled history. They had begun dating when Bruce's relationship with a beautiful young woman named Regina Morrow was breaking up. Unfortunately, Regina was so devastated by the breakup that she fell in with a crowd that used drugs. At a party one night Regina was talked into trying cocaine. She had had a terrible reaction due to an undiagnosed heart condition, and she had immediately fallen into a coma and died within hours. For weeks afterward Bruce and Amy had seen very little of each other. They dated occasionally, but that was it, and Jessica didn't expect anything serious to come out of it. As far as she was concerned, Bruce's relationship with Regina had been a fluke. Regina had been so good and loving, and for a while Bruce seemed to have changed—to be much less arrogant and selfish. But now he was back to his old antics, and Jessica didn't trust him one bit.

Lunch had been served, and everyone was having a good time, except, Jessica thought with interest, her brother Steven. In fact, Steven really didn't seem to be acting like himself. He looked handsome in a khaki cotton summer suit, but he wasn't paying much attention to Cara. Now that she'd noticed, Jessica couldn't think about anything else. Cara seemed awfully quiet, considering this was her party, and her pretty brown eyes were fixed anxiously on Steven's face.

"How's your steak?" Cara asked, putting her hand on his arm.

"Fine," Steven said, not very enthusiastically. Jessica, her eyes lowered, listened closely.

"You seem quiet," Cara observed in a low voice. "Is anything wrong?"

"I just don't feel well," Steven complained. "Would you excuse me? I'm going to the men's room. I'll be back in a minute."

Cara watched with an anxious gaze as Steven

left the table. "Jessica," she said, frowning, "has Steve been acting differently since he came home?"

"What do you mean?" Jessica asked, pretending she hadn't noticed the exchange that had just taken place. "He seems the same to me. He just sneezes a lot more."

Cara frowned. "I wonder. . . . He seems kind of distant to me." She glanced at the others. "Look, I'm going to go try to talk to him. I'll be back in a second," she said, pushing her chair back and standing. She went out to the front hall of the restaurant, intending to wait for Steven. But she didn't have to wait for him. He was sitting on a chair, scanning a piece of pink stationery, his brow wrinkled.

"Hey," Cara said with a smile, coming up behind him and putting her hands on his shoulders, "what's that? Something you don't want to read at the table?" Her voice was intimate and knowing, as if she were in on a secret with him.

Steven jumped. His face turned bright red, and he folded the stationery hastily. "Cara," he said, annoyed, "since when do you go sneaking up on people and reading over their shoulders?"

Cara felt her face grow hot. "I wasn't sneak-

49

ing!" she said indignantly. "I just came out here to see where you were, to make sure you were all right." She felt her pulse quicken. "Anyway, what difference would it make if I were looking over your shoulder? Since when do you get letters that you have to hide from me, your own girlfriend?"

"Some things are private, that's all," Steven said defensively, putting the letter into the breast pocket of his suit.

Cara was really angry now. "I don't like the way you're acting one bit," she snapped, folding her arms across her chest. "This happens to be my party, Steven. And you're barely paying attention to me! All you've done all day is complain. I know you don't feel well, but that doesn't mean you have to act as if I don't exist!"

Steven glared at her. "You're acting like a baby, Cara. I told you the night I got back, this isn't a vacation for me. I've got tons of homework to do, and I feel rotten all the time. I know I'm not acting like myself, but can't you be more sympathetic?"

Cara looked resentful. "What about the fact that it's my party? Doesn't that count?"

Steven sighed. "Look, I'm sorry," he said, putting his arm around her. "I don't know what it is. I just feel kind of out of it, that's all. Can't you bear with me for a little while until I start to feel better?"

"I guess so," Cara said. She stared at him but said nothing more.

Jessica had advised her to bring some mystery into their relationship. Well, now there was something mysterious between them—the letter Steven had been reading. But it didn't make Cara feel good at all. And from the expression on Steven's face as they made their way back to the table together, it wasn't making him feel good either.

For the rest of the party Cara was quiet and distracted, and neither she nor Steven finished their meals. Jessica watched them both with quiet fascination.

Steven and Cara usually got along so well, and Jessica had never seen them like this before. She couldn't help but wonder if she had stirred up trouble between them by suggesting that Cara act aloof. Well, there was nothing she could do about it now but wait and see what happened.

Five

Abbie frowned at herself in the mirror. It was Monday morning, and she had just finished gym class and was busily trying to straighten her hair before the bell rang. She had taken special pains getting dressed that morning, following an old piece of advice from her mother, who always said to dress nicely when she was feeling insecure. It would make Abbie feel better about herself, she assured Abbie. And in this case it did help, she had to admit. Abbie had sworn to herself that she was going to be friendly and cheerful to everyone. And she was going to go out of her way to be helpful.

The locker room door opened, and Cara and Lila came in, deep in conversation. Abbie felt her cheeks redden, but she was determined not to act flustered or silly around Cara. "Hi," she said, smiling so hard her face muscles ached. "How are you guys? Did you have a nice weekend?"

"It was OK," Cara said, opening her locker. She looked slightly embarrassed but didn't say anything about her party. Abbie didn't either. But suddenly she knew it was crazy to give Cara's present to Elizabeth. She had chosen it for Cara, hadn't she? Why not just do the simplest thing and give it to her anyway?

"I have something for you," she said to Cara, taking the small package out of her purse. "I know you had your birthday party yesterday. I meant to give you this earlier, but I didn't have a chance." The effort of smiling was beginning to get to her.

Cara looked at the package with an expression of complete mortification. "Oh, Abbie," she said, obviously so confused she had no idea what to say. "You shouldn't have done that! I mean . . ."

"It's just a little something," Abbie said, getting embarrassed herself. "It's nothing, really."

Fumbling with the wrapping paper, Cara glanced uneasily at Lila. When she opened the box, she looked more embarrassed than ever. "This is so pretty," she said, taking out the ring and slipping it on. "Abbie, this was really nice of you."

Abbie shrugged. "Well, happy belated birthday," she said, backing away uncertainly. She couldn't tell whether it had been a good idea or not to give Cara the present. She hadn't meant to make her feel uncomfortable, but that seemed to be the result. *Boy*, Abbie thought sadly, *I can't do* anything *right these days!*

Cara and Lila were silent until Abbie left the locker room. "God, I feel like such a jerk!" Cara cried, slapping her hand to her forehead. "I can't believe she gave me a present. She must have been sitting around waiting for me to call her about the party for a week. I feel so terrible I could die!"

"Oh, don't worry about it," Lila said airily, opening her locker and taking out her swimsuit. "She gave you the present, didn't she? She must not be mad at you."

Cara's face was still red from embarrassment. "That isn't the point," she said, miserable. "I obviously hurt her feelings, Lila. I wanted to drop through the floor when she wished me a happy birthday." She stared down at the ring. "God, I wish I'd just included her. It wouldn't have been such a big deal."

Lila didn't seem particularly concerned. "Abbie's the world's most forgiving person," she pointed out. "She obviously doesn't care about the party, so why should you? She's the sort of girl who doesn't get upset about *anything*."

Cara sighed. She knew Abbie was easygoing, and it was true that she never seemed to get mad. But she still felt terrible about what had happened. Especially considering how the party had turned out. She could have invited Abbie instead of Steven for all the good it had done her to spend her birthday lunch with *him*! She probably would have had a much better time without him.

"I can't believe how nice of you this is," Abbie gushed. She and Elizabeth were in the Wakefields' living room with all of Abbie's "Jenny" sketches spread out before them.

"Are you kidding? It's fun. Besides, you're the one who's doing the paper a favor. Your cartoon strip is going to send *The Oracle*'s popularity sky-high!" Elizabeth pointed out.

"Well, thanks, but I haven't won yet. Anyway, you're so nice to help me," Abbie said. Elizabeth was the first person who had really gone out of her way to make Abbie feel completely welcome since she and Doug had broken up. Elizabeth was so easy to be with, and she always had something nice to say. She made Abbie feel a lot better about herself.

"I've been helping Amy Sutton with her entry," Abbie added. "I think her idea is really cute."

Elizabeth watched Abbie as she bent over some sketches. "You've been helping Amy?" she asked incredulously. "But she's your competition! You know, Abbie, you're a funny girl," Elizabeth mused aloud. "I've never met anyone who's so giving, so willing to volunteer and do things for other people, and at the same time so reluctant to take things from people."

Abbie shrugged. "I like helping people the same way you do." She blushed a little under Elizabeth's scrutinizing gaze. Abbie remembered her mother saying to her once that she thought Abbie preferred giving to taking because it meant she could be more in control. But Abbie didn't believe that was true. She just wanted people to like her. She really felt she owed it to Amy to help her out—even if it meant jeopardizing her own chances of winning the competition.

"OK, now, which cartoon do you think you want to enter in the last stage of the contest?" Elizabeth asked, picking up one or two of Abbie's preliminary sketches.

Abbie frowned. "I'm not really sure. The thing is, I'd like to show Jenny going through a crisis of some sort. Maybe she's thinking about getting back together with her boyfriend or something. Or"—she looked intently at Elizabeth—"maybe she decides to completely change her image." She snapped her fingers. "That would be perfect! She's sick of being the old doormat Jenny and decides to come to school totally different. And then something silly can happen that shows she's still really the same."

Elizabeth was about to comment when Steven wandered into the living room. "Steve, do you know Abbie?" Elizabeth asked.

Steven nodded. "We met at your video party, Liz." He smiled at Abbie. "Don't mind me if I look like I just got over the measles. I've been going to this allergist, and he keeps shooting me full of strange substances to find out what I'm allergic to." He looked ruefully at his red arms. "I think this time he may have found out what it is."

Abbie laughed. "I'm allergic to cats," she said sympathetically. "I had to go through all those tests two years ago. They're awful, aren't they?"

"They sure are," Steven agreed, then smiled and left the room. Abbie looked at Elizabeth. "He seems like such a nice guy," she said enthusiastically. "I had forgotten you had such a cute older brother. He goes out with Cara, right?"

Elizabeth nodded. "They're actually going through some tough times right now," she confided. "I think the distance thing is starting to get to them. In fact—"

"Lizzie!" Jessica hollered from the kitchen. "Something terrible is happening to this spaghetti sauce. Can you come help me?"

"That girl," Elizabeth declared, getting to her feet. "You'd think she'd be able to cook dinner by herself for once!"

"I can help," Abbie volunteered.

"Absolutely not! You came over here to work on your cartoons, not to help Jessica make spaghetti sauce," Elizabeth chided her. "I'll be back in a second," she added, hurrying out of the room.

Steven came back in just then and looked at the sketches Abbie had been working on. "Hey, these are great!" he exclaimed. "Are you the one Liz was telling me about who does cartoons for the paper? These are absolutely terrific."

"Thanks. They're not in the paper yet. We're in the middle of a competition for the humor section of the paper, and this is what I'm submitting," Abbie said shyly. "The main character is called Jenny. She's supposed to be an average sixteen-year-old with an average sixteen-year-old's problems," she added with a smile.

Steven sat down on the couch. The truth was, he didn't really want to make small talk. He didn't feel well, and he was worried about his history term paper. Even worse was the argument he'd had with Cara the day before; it really bothered him. They didn't usually fight, and if they did, they quickly made up.

"You look worried," Abbie said quietly. "Is anything wrong?"

Steven was surprised. Most of his sisters' friends acted pretty silly around him if they talked to him at all. He hadn't realized that his tension was so apparent, and he was startled that Abbie would comment on it so openly.

"I am a little worried," he admitted. To his amazement he found himself confiding in her all in a rush. "At first I just thought it was my allergies that were bugging me, but now everything seems to be going wrong. My girlfriend—do you know Cara Walker?"

Abbie nodded.

"Well, we got into a big fight yesterday." Steven rubbed his forehead with his knuckles. "Actually, I think I acted like a real jerk. I was just feeling like I needed to be . . . I can't even put my finger on it. Something just feels strange between us. And I've got all this work to do, and I'm not feeling well. . . ." His voice trailed off, and he looked down at the carpet. Steven couldn't believe he was talking this way to a girl he barely knew.

But Abbie didn't seem fazed by anything he said. "I think everyone goes through periods when they're kind of off," she said. "Sometimes just admitting it helps. But it isn't easy if you're in a relationship. Your girlfriend probably takes your behavior personally, and that isn't how you mean it at all."

Steven brightened visibly. "You're right!" he exclaimed. "I guess I've just been feeling like I need a little time to myself to get some stuff sorted out. And she's acting so different from the way she usually does—so clingy and possessive."

"I'm sure she doesn't mean to be clingy. She's probably just worried about you," Abbie said.

"You know, you're amazingly easy to talk to," Steven said admiringly. Looking considerably more relaxed, he leaned back on the sofa. "How come I haven't seen you around here much?"

"Well, I haven't been friends with Liz for that long. She's been helping me with these cartoons. Your sister," Abbie added, "is the world's most generous person. If it weren't for her—"

"If it weren't for her, what?" Elizabeth demanded, coming back into the living room. Abbie blushed and shook her head.

"She was just raving about all your finest qualities," Steven said with a smile. He couldn't believe how much better he felt all of a sudden. In fact, he couldn't wait to go upstairs and call Cara and explain how he'd been feeling. Talking to Abbie made him realize that he was blowing the whole thing out of proportion. He had just been feeling pressured. There wasn't anything wrong between Cara and him after all.

"Listen, good luck with those cartoons," Steven said, smiling down at Abbie.

After Steven left the room, Abbie couldn't help thinking how great the Wakefield family was.

"Where are you going?" Elizabeth demanded as Abbie got to her feet.

"I want to help Jessica with the spaghetti sauce," Abbie said cheerfully. And before Elizabeth could say a word in protest, Abbie was in the kitchen, saving Jessica from certain disaster.

Abbie had every intention of coming back often to the Wakefields' house. And she was sure the best way to make them invite her back was to make herself useful.

Steven sat down at his desk. He was about to dial Cara's number when his glance fell on the corner of a piece of pink stationery sticking out of his history textbook. His mouth felt dry as he slipped the letter out of the book. It had been typed in an italic typeface.

"Dear Steve," it began.

You know how I feel about you, so this is probably silly, but I just feel like writing. Sometimes, especially when we're so far apart, writing really helps, don't you think? I can almost imagine kissing you. . . . I know you know who I am, so I'm not even going to sign this. And you know how I feel, too. In fact, my feelings for you are getting stronger all the time. My heart pounds when I think of you. All my love, always . . .

Steven frowned. He had read the letter so many times by now that he practically had it memorized. He was about to put the letter away when Elizabeth pushed open his door.

"Hey," she said, "Jessica was wondering if you wanted to come down—" She stopped short. "What's that?" she demanded, looking at the letter. "That stationery looks . . ."

Steven quickly crumpled the letter up. "Since when do you barge in here without knocking?" he demanded.

Elizabeth stared at him in disbelief. She wasn't used to her brother yelling at her. "I'm sorry," she said, backing out of the room.

"Look, Liz, *I'm* sorry," Steven amended. "It's just, well, I don't know. I feel like I don't have much privacy these days." His gaze dropped down to the offending letter again. Elizabeth looked at it, too. Even though the stationery was crumpled, she could see it was very pretty, with distinctive flowers embossed on it.

"Listen, I'll leave you alone," Elizabeth said quietly, pulling the door closed behind her.

Steven didn't answer her. He wasn't in the mood to call Cara anymore. In fact, the feeling of relief that had come over him when he talked with Abbie had almost entirely disappeared. He picked up the crumpled piece of pink stationery and smoothed it out carefully. Frowning he re-read the message again and again.

The truth was, he had no idea who had sent him the letter, but he had to find out who it was.

Six

"Abbie!" Jessica exclaimed, opening the front door and smiling at the brunette. "Come on in. Liz must be upstairs."

It was the third afternoon that week that Abbie had been at the Wakefields', and Jessica was beginning to accept the fact that she was becoming a permanent fixture around the house. More important, Jessica, in characteristic fashion, was finding ways to turn Abbie's presence to her own advantage.

In fact, Jessica was even beginning to enjoy Abbie's company. How could anyone help it? Abbie had to be the world's easiest person to get along with. If you told her a joke, she thought it was the funniest thing she'd ever heard. If you looked tired, she asked you—immediately—

what was the matter. She asked a zillion times if there was anything she could do to help you, and it didn't take Jessica long to discover that she meant it. She really *liked* doing things such as setting the table or folding the laundry or adding up some problem sets for Jessica in math.

Jessica had never met anyone quite like Abbie before. She couldn't figure her out. Abbie was extremely pretty, though she dressed more conservatively than Jessica did, especially considering she had such a good figure. Everything about Abbie seemed *nice.* She had a nice smile, a nice sense of humor, and a seemingly endless amount of patience. "There's got to be an ulterior motive," Jessica grumbled to Elizabeth when they talked about Abbie. "Why else would someone *ask* to help fold the laundry?"

"Be careful," Elizabeth warned her twin. "If you start taking advantage of Abbie, I'm going to kill you. She can't help being so nice."

But Jessica wasn't convinced yet. She was sure Abbie had to want something. It was the only thing that made sense. Jessica fully intended to find out what that something was.

"What are you doing?" Abbie wondered aloud, taking off her backpack and setting it down. She followed Jessica out onto the patio where a basket of clothes was sitting.

68

"My mom made me promise to mend these things," Jessica said, glaring at the sewing kit on the patio table. "She threatened to cut off my allowance and not let me buy a single new piece of clothing till I fixed the things that need fixing." She picked up a skirt and examined it. "I never can remember what stitch you're supposed to use when you hem a skirt."

"I can show you," Abbie volunteered automatically. "It's really easy. See, all you do is fold the bottom over like this, and then you can use the slip stitch. It's the easiest, and it doesn't show through."

"You'd better show me," Jessica said. "I'm really hopeless at this sort of thing."

In a minute Abbie had the needle threaded and was demonstrating the stitch.

But Jessica had lost interest. "Prince!" she hollered, jumping up to chase the Wakefields' golden retriever puppy across the lawn as the dog tried to run off. By the time she had rescued the puppy from invisible danger, Abbie was totally absorbed in hemming. Jessica sat down beside her, the panting, struggling puppy in her lap. "You're doing that so fast," she said enviously. "It would take me an hour to get that far."

Abbie eyed Jessica. "Why don't you let me

finish it, then? You're right, Jess. I can do this hem in five minutes."

Jessica pretended to think it over. "Are you sure, Abbie? You really don't mind?"

Abbie looked hurt. "Of course I don't mind! It's just one little hem."

"OK. I'll be right back, then. I'm just going to put Prince inside." *Boy*, Jessica thought, *Abbie Richardson is a real find.* With Abbie around, Jessica might be able to get all her chores done and still have time to lie out in the sun before dinner!

Jessica set Prince loose in the house and was about to go back outside when the phone rang. It was Lila, wanting to tell her about the incredibly cute guy she had just met downtown who claimed to have a friend who was really nice. Jessica got so intrigued in the conversation, she forgot all about Abbie. When Elizabeth came downstairs ten minutes later, Jessica was still on the phone, and Abbie was out on the patio, hard at work.

"Hi!" Elizabeth exclaimed, opening the sliding door to the patio and coming out to inspect Abbie's handiwork. "What are you doing? I didn't even know you were here."

"Jessica let me in," Abbie explained. "I'm just helping her hem this skirt. See?"

"Why are *you* doing that?" Elizabeth asked, annoyed beyond belief with her sister. "Jessica has been meaning to do that mending for about a month now. Our mom told her this morning that if she didn't get it done by tonight, she was going to lose her allowance."

"She told me that," Abbie said calmly. "But Jessica isn't much good at sewing, Liz. It would have taken her forever just to do this little hem. And I'm almost done!"

"That," Elizabeth said firmly, "is beside the point." She gave Abbie a searching look. "Listen, maybe this isn't my place, Abbie, but I've been wondering about something. Why do you always offer to do so much for other people? In some cases I can understand it. But these are Jessica's chores, and she should be doing them."

Abbie looked surprised. "But I like helping out," she said simply.

Elizabeth groped for the right thing to say. "I know you do, and I think you're one of the sweetest, most generous people I've ever met. Don't get me wrong, Abbie. It's just that sometimes it seems you go out of your way to do things you don't have to do." She frowned at the basket of clothes. "Like Jessica's sewing."

Abbie felt her face redden. "Maybe it's because I don't have any brothers or sisters," she suggested. "I guess I've never felt that anyone was taking advantage of me. I like it when people ask me to do things."

Elizabeth sat down, a serious expression on her face. "You could be right about not having sisters or brothers. That's one thing about having siblings—you learn quickly not to volunteer too much! The truth is, Abbie, people *do* take advantage—even of their friends—if they're allowed to."

"I don't see how a friend could take advantage of a friend," Abbie protested. Her silky brown hair fell softly against her cheek as she leaned over Jessica's skirt.

"Well, it's a sticky question," Elizabeth said. "I don't think people do it on purpose—it just happens. You get used to your friends being a certain way. If you knew, no matter what, that I'd always lend you money and wouldn't ever ask for it back, or even expect to get it back, wouldn't that change the way you felt about returning the loan?"

"I don't think so," Abbie said uncertainly.

Elizabeth sighed. "I'm not a cynic, Abbie. In fact, I think I expect too much of people sometimes. But I know that people who ask to be taken advantage of end up being taken advantage of. It just happens."

"Are you saying I shouldn't offer to help out?" Abbie demanded.

"Well—no, but maybe just not so much. I think you need to help yourself out more," Elizabeth said. "Jessica sure doesn't need help! That girl would have the President hem her skirt for her if he were here and willing to do it!"

Abbie blushed. "OK. Maybe you're right," she said softly. "You know, Liz, Doug used to say the same thing to me. I never really made the connection before, but he complained that I gave too much, that I made him feel guilty by giving all the time. Guilty and smothered."

Elizabeth didn't say anything for a minute. It was hard for her to get a sense of what Doug Brewster was like as a person, but she could tell that the relationship had obviously damaged Abbie's ego. The girl needed to learn how much she had to offer, how much people wanted to spend time with her because of who she was, not because of what she would do for them.

"Well, you know you're welcome here no matter what," Elizabeth said finally. "Just re-member, Abbie, you're great company. You're fun to be around, and you're incredibly sweet. That's why we're glad you come over. Now, leave that stuff alone and let Jessica worry about it!"

Abbie looked uneasily at the pile of unmended clothes in the basket. She hated to leave Jessica with so much to do.

"Abbie," Elizabeth said mock-threateningly.

"OK, OK," Abbie said with a laugh. But she couldn't help looking back guiltily at the work she had left for Jessica to finish.

"Well, they've finally figured it out. I'm allergic to a whole bunch of things—mold, dust, and grass, to name a few," Steven said with a smile. "Can you believe it? Tomorrow I get my first allergy shots, and then I start getting them once a week for the rest of my life, or something. Well, for a long time," he amended. "The doctor's also prescribed a new antihistamine, one that won't make me feel tired like the other one."

Abbie smiled. "Gosh, that's too bad you have so many allergies, but I'm sure you'll start feeling better once you start taking the shots and the pills. A lot better than you've been feeling lately anyway."

"You know, that's what I like about you, Abbie," Steven said. The two were sitting together in the living room, listening to music, waiting for Jessica and Elizabeth to get back from the store. Jessica had forgotten to buy groceries for dinner and had almost cajoled Abbie into going for her, but Elizabeth, more sternly than usual, had intercepted and dragged Jessica off herself. "You're so understanding. I just wish Cara were a little more like you."

Abbie took a small sip of iced tea. "Is she still acting funny?"

It had become part of the routine, now that she was over at the Wakefields' so much, for Abbie to sit and talk with Steven about Cara. At first Abbie hadn't even noticed how soon their conversations zeroed in on Steven's anxiety about Cara, but now she expected it. She wondered if Elizabeth would think Steven was taking advantage of her by confiding his troubles in her.

But Abbie liked Steven too much to suspect him of anything like that. She thought he was one of the nicest guys she'd ever met. And she really felt for him, too. She knew how hard it was going through a relationship that was foundering. When she and Doug decided to split up, she had been unable to work for weeks. She had lost interest in art, in classwork, even in her appearance. She could see some of her own feelings in Steven as he described the tension that was developing between Cara and him.

That day Steven seemed more on edge than usual. "Abbie, you're probably the best listener I've ever met. Would you— If I tell you something, would you promise not to tell anyone else? Not a living soul."

Abbie's eyes were very wide and blue as she stared at him. "I promise," she said promptly.

Steven put his head in his hands. He looked troubled and sad. "Did you know Tricia Martin?" he asked her.

Abbie shook her head. "I knew all about her," she said, "but I didn't know her." Everyone knew about Tricia Martin. It was one of the saddest stories Abbie had ever heard. Tricia and Steven had been going out for a long time when Tricia was diagnosed as having leukemia. She had fought bravely for her life, but in the end she could not overcome the disease. Steven had been inconsolable. Tricia's death was the hardest thing he had ever had to face. Talking about it now was clearly an effort for him.

"You know, I have to admit that her memory began to fade," he said slowly, running his fingers through his hair. "Being away at college . . . meeting Cara . . . you know how it is. Time really does heal things, as the saying goes. Then all of a sudden, just when I felt like my life was really shaping up, and I had a new girlfriend I loved"—he leaned forward intently—"I got this letter."

"A letter?" Abbie echoed, her eyes big.

Steven nodded seriously. "On Tricia's stationery. It was absolutely unmistakable, the same pink stationery she used to write me letters on. God, it was like seeing a ghost! I can't tell you how much that letter upset me."

"Did you tell Cara about it?" Abbie asked promptly.

Steven shook his head. "No. See, Cara's always been kind of funny about Tricia. It's not that Cara's jealous, but I think she feels that Tricia is a subject we just can't talk about. You know Cara's parents got divorced this year, and her father got custody of her little brother. Since then Cara's been very vulnerable, and there are certain subjects she refuses to discuss. Tricia seems to be one of them. When I got the letter . . ." He sighed. "I'm just afraid it'll start a whole scene. And Cara's been acting so strange lately, too. She seems really possessive and insecure. Any time we do anything together we end up having a fight. She claims I don't pay enough attention to her, and I end up getting really upset."

"I don't understand," Abbie mused. "Who on earth could have sent you a letter on Tricia's stationery? Who would play such a cruel joke?"

"The worst thing is, this morning I got another one on the same stationery, written on the same typewriter." Steven looked extremely upset. "Abbie, I just don't know what to do."

"I think you should tell Cara," Abbie said thoughtfully. "I don't know her very well, but I do know this: It's impossible to keep something a secret when you're in love. The harder you try, the bigger the gulf between you will grow. Cara must know there's something bugging you. And I can't believe she isn't incredibly worried about it. Maybe that's why she's acting more possessive. She must sense there's something that you aren't telling her."

Steven shook his head. "I wish you were right, Abbie. But Cara isn't acting like herself. If she were like you . . ." His voice trailed off, and he looked straight at Abbie, whose heart began to pound.

"Uh, that must be Jessica and Liz," Abbie said quickly, getting to her feet as she heard their car pull up the driveway.

Steven reddened. "I didn't mean to embarrass you, Abbie. I just want you to know how grateful I am for your support. You're a good friend."

Abbie blushed deeply. For the first time she realized how much she enjoyed these conversations with Steven. Was she really just being a supportive listener, or was there something more involved in her feelings for Steven?

"Hey, we got some of the new gourmet ice cream Lila's been telling me about," Jessica called, hurrying into the room with the groceries. She stopped short when she saw her brother and Abbie together.

"Am I interrupting something?" she said in a silky voice.

"No!" Steven and Abbie said in unison, both red-faced.

Jessica raised her eyebrows and went to the kitchen to put the ice cream in the freezer. Something in Abbie's expression made her feel distinctly uneasy. Suppose she were right about Abbie after all. Suppose the girl really *did* have an ulterior motive.

And suppose, just suppose, that the ulterior motive had something to do with Steven.

Seven

"Hey, look!" Penny exclaimed, opening up the folder of final entries for *The Oracle*'s humor feature. "Abbie's submitted her final version of the 'Jenny' cartoon strip!" She called Elizabeth over to take a look.

The strip had come out beautifully, each black-and-white sketch a perfect accompaniment to the text Abbie had written. There were four panels. In the first panel Jenny was listening to a long harangue about being more independent and assertive. A TV commentator was describing a course that could help someone become "your own person." In the second panel Jenny was thinking to herself that she could use such a course. "That's exactly what I ought to do! Everyone tells me I ought to be more independent." In the third panel she looked confused as she said, "But how am I going to get to the Assertiveness Training Center?" In the fourth panel Jenny was on the phone to Mel, her boyfriend, saying, "Mel, will you drive me to the Assertiveness Training Center so I won't have to rely on you so much anymore?"

"Abbie's great at this!" Penny said, giggling at the cartoon. "She's really done an excellent job. She has a good sense of humor, too. Don't you think so, Liz? This is really funny."

Elizabeth nodded in agreement. "But where's Amy's Miss Manners spin-off?" she asked. The entries were due that day at noon, and it was already ten minutes after the hour.

Penny frowned. "You're not going to believe this, but I actually saw Abbie helping Amy with the finishing touches last hour. Doesn't that seem a little above and beyond the call of duty? Why would Abbie want to help Amy when she's her competition?"

Elizabeth sighed and shook her head. "I think Abbie shares some of Jenny's problems," she remarked. "I don't know why she's so eager to help other people all the time, but sometimes she seems to get in her own way."

Just then the door to the *Oracle* office swung open, and Amy Sutton stuck her head inside.

"Ooops," she said, staring at Elizabeth and Penny. "I guess I'm a teeny bit late with my entry. But you guys don't mind, do you?" She sneaked a manila envelope onto Penny's desk. "It's finally just the way I want it," she added breathlessly.

"Did Abbie really help you with it?" Elizabeth asked her directly.

Amy shrugged. "A little bit. But so what? The idea is all mine. And I think it's tons better than her stupid comic strip."

"That's a nice way to talk," Penny said, "after Abbie's knocked herself out helping you."

But Amy Sutton wasn't one to feel bad about anything. "Look," she said, fluffing up her blond hair, "I didn't force the girl to help me. She wanted to. When do you choose who wins the contest?" she asked breathlessly. "I can't wait to find out!"

"Well, Mr. Collins is making the final decision over the weekend. I guess we'll know on Monday," Penny said slowly. She and Elizabeth watched Amy bounce out the door, and they exchanged anxious glances. Neither Penny nor Elizabeth would have any say in who won the contest. Mr. Collins was going to make the final decision. But it was clear they both felt the same way. Abbie really ought to be the winner.

The question was, why was Abbie so reluctant to champion herself? And why had she actually gone out of her way to help Amy Sutton win the contest?

Cara was poking listlessly at her salad, a pout on her pretty face. She was sitting with Lila and Jessica, but she seemed a thousand miles away.

"Cara," Lila said, putting down her fork and looking at Cara with her ultrasophisticated I-know-what's-good-for-you expression. "Is something wrong with you? You look like you just lost every share of stock you own."

Jessica laughed. "Only you, Lila, would describe depression in terms of a market crash. How about saying she looks like she just lost her best friend?"

Lila ignored this jab. "Seriously, Cara. You haven't said a word all lunch hour. And you're not eating."

"I'm not hungry," Cara said quietly. "And I don't really feel like talking, that's all."

"Uh-oh," Lila said. "This sounds like love trouble."

Cara's eyes filled with tears. "I don't want to talk about it!" she snapped. "Can't you two just leave me alone?"

Jessica and Lila exchanged concerned glances. "Look, Cara," Jessica said, patting her awkwardly on the shoulder, "this sounds really serious. You know how rotten you're going to feel if you keep it bottled up."

"Besides, we can give you good advice," Lila pointed out. "Isn't that what friends are for?"

"I can't talk about it," Cara said sadly. "Anyway, Jessica, you're Steve's sister. I can't expect you to sit and listen to me say rotten stuff about him."

Jessica's eyebrows shot up. "Rotten things—about Steve? Is this the same Cara who wouldn't let me even suggest that you two weren't Romeo and Juliet the Second?" Jessica was pretty sure she could stand to hear rotten things about her brother—at least she was curious enough to want to know what they were.

"Well, we've been having some problems," Cara said at last. "I'm not sure exactly what's wrong, but all of a sudden we just can't seem to talk to each other."

"Start at the beginning," Lila advised. "Do you think he's seeing someone else? Maybe someone at school?"

"Steven wouldn't cheat on Cara," Jessica said defensively. Now that her curiosity was partly satisfied, family loyalty was returning. She felt obliged to stick up for her brother.

Lila didn't appear convinced. "Look, Jess, we know he's your brother and everything, but he's still a guy. A college guy at that. It's only logical that he'd be tempted. Think of all those gorgeous girls up there on the beaches . . . all those parties—"

"Lila," Cara interrupted, burying her face in her hands, "you're not exactly helping matters."

"Well, unless you tell us what's going on, how can we help?" Lila pointed out.

"OK," said Cara, sighing. "All I know is that he's been acting like a totally different person since he's been home. At first I thought it was just because he wasn't feeling well, and he was having all those tests. But you know Steve! Usually he's the world's sweetest, most considerate guy. He'd never do anything to hurt my feelings. He always tries to make me feel like the center of his world. But since he's been home—" She bit her lip. "He barely even seems to notice me when we're together. He doesn't even act affectionate anymore, doesn't try to hold my hand or snuggle with me on the couch or anything." She looked despairingly at Jessica and Lila. "I don't think he loves me anymore!" she burst out, the tears spilling down her face.

"Poor Cara," Lila said sympathetically. "You're obviously getting phased out of the picture. No wonder you've been so quiet. You've been suffering all alone, and we didn't even know!"

Jessica was absolutely riveted. "Tell us more," she insisted. "What do you mean he doesn't seem to notice you when you're together? Does it seem like he's thinking about someone else?"

"Or someone else?" Lila echoed darkly.

Cara wiped the tears from her eyes. "I don't know," she said slowly. "It's . . . well, to tell you the truth, it's like he's being secretive about something. Like there's something that he can't tell me about. Maybe there *is* someone else. That would make sense, I guess, because whenever I try to ask him about how he's feeling, he just looks quiet and upset, like he wants me to leave him alone. I can't believe it." She shook her head ruefully. "Jess, remember when I was telling you recently how open he and I are with each other?" She laughed bitterly. "Well, I was completely wrong. Whatever's going on, we're not being honest with each other at all. I can't even tell him how upset I am."

"Why not?" Jessica asked reasonably. "How are you supposed to find out what's wrong if you can't talk to him about it? Why don't you just ask him straight out what's going on?"

Cara shook her head vehemently. "You don't understand. The only way to straighten things out is to play things his way, to back off and act like I'm as disinterested as he is. That way maybe he'll have to try harder to win me back again."

"Well, I don't really know that much about serious relationships," Jessica said slowly, "but that sounds crazy to me. I think you should just talk to him, Cara. Maybe you two are making a big deal out of nothing."

Lila looked appalled. "No way! Cara is absolutely right, Jess. Do exactly what you said, Cara," she instructed. "Make sure you're as distant and unavailable as you can possibly be. It wouldn't even hurt to break a couple of dates, maybe show up late, that sort of thing. That ought to make him nervous!"

Jessica shook her head. "You're nuts," she said.

But Lila wasn't about to be interrupted. "Steven just needs to realize that he can't take you for granted," she said with authority. "Once he's learned his lesson, you'll never have to worry about this again."

Cara stared at the table and twisted her napkin unhappily, wishing she were as sure of the right approach as Lila seemed to be. Her relationship with Steven was becoming more and more troubling, and the truth was, she didn't have the faintest idea of what to do to make things as good as they had been before.

Frowning, Abbie rang the Wakefields' door bell for the second time. It was four o'clock. Hadn't Elizabeth said to come by between three-thirty and four?

At last the door opened, and Steven looked at her with surprise, temporary confusion, and pleasure. "Abbie! Come on in," he said.

Abbie stared past him into the front hall. "I—uh, I was supposed to get together with Liz," she said awkwardly. "Is she home?"

"She's working late at *The Oracle*. And Jessica has cheerleading. But it doesn't matter. I'm here," Steven said, smiling broadly. "Come on in and keep me company while you wait for them."

Abbie blushed. Why hadn't she remembered that Elizabeth was working late on the paper? Steven must think she was a total flake, or that she'd forgotten on purpose. How completely embarrassing!

But within minutes Steven had made her feel totally relaxed. Soon the two of them were sitting out on the patio, drinking iced tea and talking.

"Any more letters?" Abbie asked him.

Steven shook his head. "No, but the mail hadn't come yet when I looked. To tell you the truth, I'm almost afraid to check."

"I don't blame you. It sounds so creepy," Abbie agreed. She was quiet for a minute. "How are things otherwise?"

"You mean with Cara?" Steven looked out at the clear water of the pool. "Well, not great, to tell you the truth. I don't know what to do, Abbie." He leaned forward and stared at her intently. "I bet you could give me sound advice. You seem like you've got such a good head on your shoulders."

"Who, me?" Abbie faltered. "Are you kidding? I'm the last person to give anyone advice. Except I do think you should try to talk to her," she said slowly.

"You're right," Steven said softly, still looking straight at her. "The problem is, I just don't think Cara and I have the ability to talk to each other anymore. One thing I've learned from all the discussions we've had is how important it is to be able to say what's on my mind. I just can't do that with Cara anymore."

Abbie felt her face flush with color. She didn't

know what to say. Suddenly she felt incredibly confused, and it occurred to her that she really liked Steven. Not just as a friend, either. For the first time since Doug, she had started to have feelings for someone. She could barely admit to herself that it was true, but she was starting to think about Steven all the time. She liked everything about him—his looks, his sense of humor, his relaxed, mature attitude. One thing was clear, though. However much Steven enjoyed talking to her, he was still attached to Cara. And Abbie would never trespass on that commitment. She felt she owed it to Steven and to Cara to encourage him to open up to Cara.

She was about to urge Steven once more to talk to Cara when, to her utter astonishment, Steven leaned over and put his hand on her arm. Just then she heard a door scrape behind her, and Elizabeth emerged from the house. Steven jumped back, his face flaming.

"Hey," Elizabeth said, setting her books down on the patio table. "This is a surprise!" She gave Abbie a startled smile, but she looked puzzled as she glanced from her brother back to her new friend.

"I—uh, I forgot you had a meeting," Abbie said weakly, feeling like a prize idiot. If only she didn't have such a fair complexion. She turned tomato-red every time she got embarrassed.

But Elizabeth seemed to have something else on her mind. "Steve, there's a letter for you," she said, taking out the mail she had picked up on her way in. She handed him the pink envelope and watched for his reaction. It was on the same stationery he had crumpled up the day Elizabeth had burst into his room without knocking.

"Thanks," Steven said, his face impassive. Trying to look unconcerned, he slipped the letter between the pages of the book he had set down on the table. But Elizabeth saw that his fingers were trembling.

Something peculiar was going on, there was no doubt about it. For one thing, why did that stationery look so familiar? And why was Steven acting so secretive about the letters? It wasn't like him at all.

Elizabeth was baffled. And something else was bothering her as well. The patio doors were made entirely of glass, and as she had crossed the dining room, Elizabeth had had a perfect view of Abbie and Steven. She couldn't hear them speaking, but she saw the looks on their faces. She had seen Steven touch Abbie's arm, and she had seen the look on Abbie's face.

That look alone was enough to alert her that something was happening between them. She wasn't sure exactly what, but she was convinced now that Abbie wasn't coming over so often just to get help on her comic strip or to get to know the twins better.

As for Steven, he didn't seem to be a detached observer. His feelings were written all over his face. Elizabeth knew her brother well enough to know that something strange was going on.

Eight

"OK," Jessica said, walking into Elizabeth's room after dinner and fixing her twin in a steely gaze, "are you going to tell me what's wrong, or are you going to sit there looking like something's driving you absolutely crazy?"

Elizabeth sighed. She was sitting at the table she used for a desk, trying to do her homework. She had been having trouble concentrating, however. The more she thought about Steven and those letters, the more worked up she became.

"OK," she said finally. "I'll tell you what's bugging me if you swear—and I mean *swear*—not to say a single word to Steve about it."

"I swear," Jessica said promptly, her eyes big

and round as she sat on the edge of Elizabeth's bed.

"Have you noticed how weird Steven's been acting lately?" Elizabeth asked.

Jessica nodded. "Yeah. Cara's been talking about it nonstop. I don't think things are so great between the two of them. Do you think Steven's met someone else?"

"Well, I don't know," Elizabeth said, frowning. "But I do know one thing. Someone's been sending him letters—on very feminine-looking stationery."

"Are you serious?" Jessica shrieked, jumping to her feet. "Liz, why didn't you tell me? What kind of letters? How come you knew and I didn't?"

Elizabeth put her fingers to her lips. "Shhh. Steve can't find out I'm telling you, or he'll kill me. I've only seen two, though there may be more, for all I know." She frowned. "I might not even have noticed. In fact, I probably would've just assumed the first letter was from Cara, except the stationery. . . . There's something strange about it. For some reason it made me think—" She shook her head, perplexed.

"Made you think what?" Jessica prompted her.

"It sounds nuts, but it looked really familiar.

What's that French term for the feeling you have when you think you've experienced something before?"

"*Déjà vu*," Jessica said. "But you couldn't think where you'd seen it?"

Elizabeth shook her heard. "Steve acted really jumpy when I came in the room. He got mad at me for not knocking, which isn't like him either. That's partly why I looked so hard at the letter."

Jessica's eyes flashed. "It's obviously from another girl," she said triumphantly. "I can't believe him! No wonder he's been acting so weird around Cara. He's just racked with guilt, that's all."

"Maybe we shouldn't jump to conclusions," Elizabeth said warily.

But telling Jessica not to jump to conclusions wasn't going to do much good. Jessica was already as suspicious as she could be. "You don't think Abbie has a crush on Steve, do you?" she demanded suddenly.

Elizabeth thought of the scene she had witnessed earlier. "Uh—why?" she said, trying to hide her discomfort. "What makes you say that?"

"Just the way she's been hanging around here all the time lately, that's all. She looks at Steve like he's some kind of Greek god or something."

Elizabeth shook her head. She saw no reason to share her misgivings with Jessica. Not at this stage. If Jessica thought Abbie liked Steven, she'd make the poor girl suffer. And Elizabeth intended to try to protect Abbie from that kind of grief.

"Girls," Mrs. Wakefield said later that evening, "will you do me a favor? I need these invitations I bought from the Pen and Paper shop exchanged. I know you were planning on going to the mall tonight to do some shopping. Could you just drop in and exchange the invitations for me?"

The twins nodded. They were going to the Midnight Madness sale at the mall. Jessica wanted a new pair of jeans, and Elizabeth was going along to keep her company. It wouldn't take long to do the errand for their mother, and as long as they were at the Pen and Paper shop, one of Elizabeth's favorite stores in the mall, she might even buy some new notebooks for journal writing.

Half an hour later the girls parked the Fiat in the mall parking lot. "Let's get Mom's errand over with first," Jessica said, heading toward the stationery store. Elizabeth followed her, her mind still buzzing with the events of the last few days.

Jessica exchanged her mother's invitations while Elizabeth looked around for the notebooks she liked. As she scanned the shelves, her eyes caught sight of a box of stationery almost exactly like the stationery Steven's letters had been typed on. "Jessica!" Elizabeth hissed. "Look at this!" She showed her twin the paper.

"What is it?" Jessica asked blankly.

"It's the same stationery that Steve's been getting in the mail—only blue. I wonder . . ."

Jessica, picked up the box and scrutinized it. "Forget-me-nots," she read aloud from the side of the box. "You know, this looks familiar, you're right. But I can't think why."

"Can I help you, girls?" a salesgirl asked, coming over to where they were standing.

"No, thanks," Elizabeth said quickly.

But Jessica wasn't about to let an opportunity like this pass her by. "Actually," she said, handing the salesgirl the box of light blue stationery, "we were looking for this same stationery in pink. Do you have any in stock?" Elizabeth could see her twin's mind was racing.

The salesgirl frowned. "I think . . . I'm pretty sure we sold the last box of pink a couple of weeks ago."

"Really?" Jessica said innocently. Elizabeth could tell her mind was racing as she tried to manufacture a plausible fib. "My sister and I want to buy this for a good friend, but we're afraid she may have bought it for herself already," she lied. "Would you mind telling us if a girl our age bought it?"

Elizabeth had to admire Jessica's ability to think on her feet. The salesgirl looked reflective. "I think it *was* a girl about your age," she said finally. "I'm not positive, though. It was a couple of weeks ago, and we see so many people in here every day. But I do happen to remember this particular sale, because it was the last box of pink, and I had to make a note of it. She was . . . oh, about your height. I can't remember much else."

"Brown hair?" Jessica demanded.

The salesgirl looked confused. "Maybe. I just remember she had a nice sweet voice. She wanted something 'romantic,' she said. I helped her choose the forget-me-not line," she added.

"Well, thanks a lot," Jessica said. "Come on," she added, turning back to her twin. "Let's go." She had a tense, excited tone in her voice that suggested she had figured something out.

"I don't get it," Elizabeth said when they were out of the store.

"Liz, it's crystal clear!" Jessica exclaimed, dragging her twin to one of the exits. "Don't you see? The whole thing makes absolutely perfect sense."

"Well, why don't you make it even clearer," Elizabeth said grouchily, following her twin out to the parking lot. "Hey, I thought you wanted to go shopping. How come we're leaving already?"

"Because we have some important things to talk about—Abbie Richardson, for instance," Jessica said, as they got in the car. She turned the key in the ignition and started driving away from the mall. "Don't you get it, Liz? In the past couple of weeks Steven suddenly starts getting these letters from a stranger on romantic pink stationery. And Abbie suddenly just happens to start hanging around our house every day, looking at Steve like he's the most wonderful thing she's ever laid eyes on. And Cara says Steve's acting weird—really distant and secretive. It all adds up perfectly!"

"You mean . . ." Elizabeth said, letting her words trail off. She stared out the window. "But Abbie's been coming over to the house because of her comic strip and because she wants to get to know us. Not because of Steve." But even as she spoke she remembered the looks on Steven's and Abbie's faces when she had spotted them through the patio doors that afternoon. "I guess you could be right," she muttered. "But I can't believe Abbie would do something like that. She seems so incredibly open and good-natured. Somehow sending love letters doesn't really seem like her style."

"Love," Jessica said portentously, "changes everything."

"Well, I hope it isn't Abbie," Elizabeth said without conviction. She couldn't bear to think the girl had just been using her as a way to get closer to Steven. Was it possible Elizabeth had misjudged her so completely?

"I want to stop and get a soda, OK?" Jessica said, pulling over at a small pharmacy that was on their way home.

"Sure," Elizabeth said absently. She was deep in thought, going over every conversation she had had with Abbie lately, trying to convince herself that Jessica was wrong. In fact, she was so deep in thought that she almost bumped smack into Betsy Martin before she recognized her.

"Betsy!" she exclaimed. "What are you doing in town?"

Betsy Martin, Tricia's younger sister, was attending an art school in L.A. After Tricia's death,

Betsy had moved in with the Wakefields for a while and still felt enormous appreciation for the way they had helped her to get on her feet again. She had been very troubled before, and her own family offered her no support after her sister's death. Betsy was a kind of adopted cousin in the Wakefield household, and Elizabeth was surprised to see she had come home without calling them.

"Didn't Steve tell you I was coming in? Actually, he's most of the reason I came back." Jessica had come over and joined them. She listened intently to what Betsy had to say. "He called me last week, really upset. He wanted to know where my dad had put all of Tricia's belongings after the funeral."

The twins exchanged anxious glances. "Belongings? What do you mean?"

"He asked about a bunch of stuff. Records, clothes—he was particularly worried about her stationery."

Elizabeth's eyes widened. Tricia's stationery. Of course! No wonder the pink paper had looked so familiar!

"Are you OK?" Betsy asked, putting her hand on Elizabeth's arm. "You look like you just saw a ghost."

Elizabeth didn't answer. Someone was sending Steven love letters on Tricia's old stationery. But who? Who could possibly do something so incredibly cruel?

Jessica and Elizabeth were up for hours that night, conferring on the mysterious letters. "I still think it's Abbie," Jessica insisted. "You heard what the girl in the stationery store said. *She* was the one who suggested the pink forget-me-not stuff. Not Abbie. It's just a weird coincidence, that's all."

"Forget-me-not," Elizabeth said with a shudder. "Ugh. It's so spooky!"

"I don't think it's spooky. I think Abbie's the only ghost around here." Jessica grimaced. "If Cara finds out, she may really be a ghost before long, because Cara will probably kill her!"

"Don't you think you're jumping to conclusions?" Elizabeth demanded. "The girl in the store didn't say it was a brunette, you did. It could have been anyone. It could just have been someone buying stationery who had nothing to do with this whole mess."

"Well, I think we should keep a close eye on Steve. I'm sure now that we know what to look for we should be able to tell. If he's in love with Abbie, it'll show," Jessica announced.

Elizabeth was quiet. She just didn't want Jessica's surmisal to be true. She *liked* Abbie Richardson. She didn't want to think Abbie had been using her to get to know Steven better!

"Girls! Steven! Can you come down for a minute?" Mrs. Wakefield called up the stairs. "Your father has some great news for you."

The twins looked at each other. "OK, now watch him carefully, Liz," Jessica hissed as they hurried downstairs to find out what was going on.

"Bob Young just called me," Mr. Wakefield said when the whole family was assembled. Bob Young was a partner of Mr. Wakefield's at the law firm. "He's got six extra tickets to the Lakers game this Saturday night."

Everyone cheered. The Lakers were facing the Celtics in the play-offs, and it was bound to be a wonderful game.

"Wait, did you say six tickets?" Jessica said. "But there're only five of us."

"Well, I thought Steve might want the extra ticket. Isn't Cara still a basketball fan?" Mr. Wakefield said, putting his arm around Steven and giving him a smile.

For once Jessica didn't complain about Steven getting preferential treatment. She was too busy studying her brother's reaction.

"Well, actually—" Steven looked uncomfortable. "Cara and I are sort of having an argument right now. I don't think she'd want to come along."

No one spoke for a minute. "Honey, is it anything serious?" Mrs. Wakefield asked, concerned.

Steven shrugged. "No. We're just—having a few problems lately." His face cleared. "I know what. Why don't we give the extra ticket to Abbie Richardson? She'd probably love to come along, don't you think?" He looked appealingly at the twins.

Jessica nudged Elizabeth so hard in the side that Elizabeth yelped. Everyone turned to look at her, and she blushed. "That sounds great," she said weakly.

She knew what Jessica was thinking. And Elizabeth had to admit that it seemed as though Jessica's theory was proving to be right.

"Well, it's your ticket," Mr. Wakefield said, clearing his throat. "Abbie's welcome to join us. And if you want to talk, at any point, about what's going on with you and Cara . . ."

Steven squirmed under his parents' scrutiny. "There's nothing wrong, I promise. Cara and I just need a little more space," he said at last.

Jessica gave her sister a triumphant look. "I

told you so," she muttered a little later as she squeezed past her on her way upstairs.

Elizabeth didn't answer. As far as she could tell, there was nothing left to say.

Nine

"I can't believe it," Lila gasped. "You mean Steven's actually taking Abbie to the basketball game instead of Cara?"

Jessica nodded solemnly. "He called her up last night right after my dad told us about the tickets. You should have heard how excited Abbie was. We could practically hear her shrieking right through the phone. It was *awful*."

Lila, who was wearing her latest pair of designer sunglasses, and Jessica were eating lunch together out on the patio next to the school cafeteria. Lila took off her sunglasses and stared at Jessica. "Does Cara know?" she demanded.

"No, I don't think so. And, Lila, you'd better not tell her. For one thing, Steve would tear me limb from limb. I don't know exactly what's going on between them, but I swore to him last night that I wouldn't talk to Cara about him."

Lila frowned. "Still," she objected, "it doesn't seem very fair to Cara. For all we know she may just be pining away on Saturday night while you're all off having a great time watching the Lakers."

"Lila," Jessica said warningly, "if you say *one word* to Cara, I'm going to kill you."

"OK, OK," Lila said hastily. "Tell me more about Abbie. You think she's been pushing this whole thing with Steve?"

"Of course she has!" Jessica exclaimed. "Why else would Steve be interested in her? She's obviously thrown herself at him. I can't say anything yet, but I'm going to get back at her, for Cara's sake." Jessica glowered. "I can't believe that rotten brother of mine would do something like this to her."

"Well, maybe it isn't all so one-sided. Maybe Cara's partly to blame, too."

Jessica gave Lila a despairing look. "Lila, you know Cara. She's totally in love with Steve. She'd do anything for him. And up until Abbie entered the picture, Steve felt the same way." She bit her lower lip. "It's obvious, Lila. Abbie's the one getting in between them. I can't believe the things that girl's been willing to stoop to!"

"Like what?" Lila asked.

"Well, she's obviously just been using Liz and me to get to know Steve. It makes me so mad to think about all the time she spent over at our house pretending she wanted to be friends with us when all she wanted was to hang out with Steve. Now I know the real reason. Abbie just wants to replace her old boyfriend, and it's clear who she's chosen to fit the bill!"

"Uh-oh," Lila said. "Here comes Cara."

Jessica looked stricken. "I'm not going to be able to stand it," she said. "It'll be way too hard for me to sit here and have to make small talk with her when I know everything I know. Lila, I'm going to run. Swear you won't repeat a single thing we said."

"I swear," Lila said automatically, putting her sunglasses back on as Jessica dashed off.

"What's with Jessica? I wanted to talk to her," Cara said, looking annoyed. She set her tray down but didn't seem particularly interested in her lunch.

"She had to find Robin Wilson to tell her something about cheerleading practice," Lila fibbed.

Cara sighed heavily. She picked up her sandwich, inspected it, then set it down again. "I can't eat," she said finally, looking miserable.

"Lila, you've got to tell me what to do. Steve and I had the biggest fight yesterday that we've ever had. It was absolutely horrible. And now I don't even know if we're ever going to talk to each other again!"

Lila studied her manicured nails with great absorption. This was going to be harder than she had expected. "What was the fight about?" she asked, trying to keep her voice neutral.

"Oh, *I* don't know. It started the way all our fights start lately. I called Steve to see how he was feeling. He said he was fine. I could tell he didn't really want to talk to me, and my feelings got hurt, so I asked him if I could come over. He said he was busy, he wanted to get his history paper done, and maybe he could come over tomorrow night instead. Well, I couldn't stand it anymore, and I asked him what was bugging him. He told me I was being way too sensitive and he just needed a little time to himself. I said that he'd been saying that all the time lately—which he has—and I didn't think we could go on this way without sitting down and figuring out what was going wrong between us."

"Hmmmm," Lila said, still studying her nails. "So what did he say to that?"

"Well, he got really defensive." Cara was about

to burst into tears. "He said that he didn't understand why I had to keep blowing everything out of proportion when all he wanted was an afternoon and evening to himself." She sighed heavily. "Maybe he's right. Maybe I'm being too demanding. After all, he hasn't been feeling very well. And besides—"

"Cara," Lila interrupted, "that's insane. Why would Steve suddenly need time for himself? He's never been that way before, has he?"

"But this is different," Cara said, beginning to defend him in earnest now. "Now I think I was being a total jerk. I mean, Steve's right! All I've been doing lately is complaining about his lack of attention. I complain that he isn't giving me enough time, I complain that he's being too quiet, I complain—"

"Stop!" Lila cried, covering her ears with her hands. "Cara, I think you have every right to complain! I think Steve's treating you like dirt. And if you ask me, the only thing to do is dump him. Fast. You can do much better anyway. Did I tell you about the gorgeous guy I met at the club?"

"I don't want a gorgeous guy at the club," Cara said mournfully. "I want Steve!"

"Well, you'll have to forget about Steve. He's

obviously got other things on his mind," Lila said briskly.

Cara set her chin stubbornly. "I'm going to call him up today and apologize," she declared. "I'm sick of all this nonsense. Deep down I love him like crazy, and I know he loves me. Isn't that all that matters?"

Lila stared at her in horror. Suddenly the promise she had made to Jessica lost its importance. She couldn't let her very good friend crawl back to Steven, knowing what she knew! "Cara, you can't do that," she said quietly.

"Why not? Why are you looking at me that way? Do you know something I don't know?" Cara demanded.

"Steven," Lila said slowly, "is taking Abbie Richardson to the Lakers game with his family on Saturday night instead of you. Now, how's that for a guy who suddenly needs so much time for himself?"

Cara stared at Lila in horror, her face turning completely white. "Are you serious?" she gasped.

Lila nodded. "Absolutely. Jessica just told me. But she made me swear not to tell you," she added uneasily. "Cara, you'd better not tell a soul. Don't you dare tell Steve. If you do, Jessica's going to know I told you."

Cara's eyes blazed with anger. "I couldn't

care less who told you what! You'd better believe I'm going to tell Steve." She was so angry and upset she was trembling violently. "I'm going to go over to his house and tell him what a jerk I think he is!" Her dark eyes filled with tears. "I'm going to kill them all," she muttered. "I bet Liz is behind this somehow. She's the one who started inviting Abbie over all the time. I bet she wanted this to happen all along!"

"Cara, please," Lila begged. "Just wait till you cool down a little before you go over and make a scene!"

"Forget it," Cara said, her teeth clenched. "I'm not keeping quiet another minute. I intend to find out exactly what's going on between Steve and Abbie. If you think I'm just going to sit back and watch her steal my boyfriend right out from under my nose, you've got another thing coming!"

And with that, Cara stomped away from the table. Lila couldn't remember ever seeing Cara so angry and upset.

"I'm really glad you can come to the game tomorrow night," Steve said to Abbie. They were sitting in the Wakefields' living room together, neither paying attention to the TV show

115

they had turned on while they waited for Elizabeth to get home. She had gone to the Dairi Burger with Jeffrey after school.

Abbie fiddled nervously with her bracelet. She felt suddenly shy around Steven. Up until their talk the day before, she had never felt so entirely at ease with a guy before. Steven was like the older brother she had never had. She felt she could tell him anything. She could relax and be entirely herself with him.

But now things had taken a different turn, and there was no denying that she felt uncomfortable. For starters, she had actually worried about what to wear that day. Usually Abbie didn't give much thought to her clothing. But that morning she had spent ages going through her closet until she finally selected a pair of designer jeans and a new hand-knit sweater. She had tried her hair in two different styles before deciding on a loose french braid. And she had added some charcoal pencil under her lower lashes. She almost *never* wore makeup.

Steven was acting differently, too. He sat up stiffly, didn't meet her gaze, and blushed at weird moments. There was no doubt about it. Something had changed between them. Abbie didn't really know what to think about it. In fact, she was feeling pretty confused.

116

She liked Steven. The truth was, she liked him a lot. He was, in some ways, everything she could have wanted in a boy—a little older, more experienced, with a wonderful mixture of gentleness and humor that really appealed to her. She found it fascinating talking to him. And in her heart she knew that if Cara were really and truly out of the picture, she would be interested.

But Cara wasn't out of the picture, yet. She might never be. And Abbie felt strongly that she mustn't do anything to sway Steven. Abbie couldn't imagine flirting with Steven, let alone really dating him, as long as he was involved with someone else. She knew too well how much it could hurt when that happened. Doug had started going out with a girl named Mariel when he and Abbie were still in the process of breaking up. Though Abbie had known deep down that the relationship was over, it hurt her even more to see Doug with another girl.

"The game will be fun. But I'm surprised you didn't ask Cara," Abbie said directly.

Steven frowned. "I appreciate your honesty, Abbie. That's one of the things I like best about you. I can really talk to you, tell you exactly what's on my mind. The sad truth is, I can't talk to Cara anymore. We just seem to misunderstand each other completely. I think we're really on the verge of breaking up."

Abbie cleared her throat. This was a hard moment for her. Partly she wanted to stay quiet, or encourage Steven in some way to follow through with this plan. If he broke up with Cara, he'd be free to date *her*. But Abbie couldn't be so selfish. Something told her that Steven wasn't saying what he really felt, and she just didn't believe it was really over between them. "Look," she said gently, "couples often go through rough periods when they can't talk to each other openly. It's scary, but it's normal. And sometimes they can't set things straight again. But sometimes it's just a problem that stems from a series of misunderstandings or from blowing things out of proportion. Don't you think that's what happened between you two?"

Steven rubbed his face unhappily. "Maybe," he said.

"Have you told Cara about the letters yet?" Abbie continued.

"No, I can't bring myself to do it." Steven took a letter out of his pocket. "Look at this! It's the fourth one. I got it today."

Abbie scanned the letter with a frown. "Boy," she said, "whoever is writing these letters really knows you pretty well. This seems to be about what's going on with you and Cara. All this stuff about growing distant and drifting apart."

"See, I'm afraid to show the letters to her for just that reason. And besides, she might freak out about the fact that it's Tricia's stationery. If only she'd be as patient and open-minded as you are, Abbie. . . ."

Abbie laughed. "Remember," she warned him, "People always look different when you're not in love with them. Especially when you're going through a rocky time with the person you *are* in love with. It's the old grass is always greener idea."

"Abbie, you're terrific," Steven said admiringly. He patted her on the arm. "Listen, I have to run upstairs for a second. Wait for me here, OK? I'll be right back."

Abbie nodded as he hurried out of the room. She was still holding the letter in her hand.

Just then the front door opened, and Jessica walked into the living room. She stood in silence for a moment, staring at the letter in Abbie's hand.

"What's that?" she asked finally, stepping closer and still staring.

Abbie's hand began to tremble. "N-nothing,"

she said weakly. Jessica inched even closer to get a better look at the piece of pink stationery.

"It can't be nothing," she said reasonably.

Abbie looked pale. "It's just a letter." And before Jessica could get any closer, Abbie folded it up and stuffed it into her bag. She wasn't going to betray Steven's confidence by saying the letter belonged to him.

Jessica looked at her without a word. Her expression as she studied the brunette was somewhere between anger and fascination. She grunted softly, then turned and strode out of the room.

Ten

Jessica was pacing up and down the driveway, waiting for Elizabeth to get home. Her hands were clasped behind her back, and her eyes were blazing. "Where is she?" she kept muttering. She couldn't help thinking that this whole mess was Elizabeth's fault. Wasn't Elizabeth the one who had started inviting Abbie over all the time? Elizabeth had introduced Abbie to Steven and encouraged them to become friendly.

And now look what had happened!

"Thank God," Jessica muttered between clenched teeth as Jeffrey's car pulled up into the driveway. She waited impatiently as Elizabeth kissed Jeffrey goodbye and got out of his car.

"What are you doing?" Elizabeth demanded,

surprised. "Are you waiting for someone, or are you just walking back and forth for exercise?"

Jessica glared at her twin. "For your information, I happen to be waiting for *you*. We have a full-blown catastrophe going on in there, and you're just sitting out here taking your sweet time, saying goodbye to Jeffrey as if you aren't ever going to see him again."

Elizabeth stared at her. It wasn't like Jessica to sound so bitter and upset. "What's wrong?" she demanded, slinging her book bag over her shoulder.

"It's Steve. And Abbie," Jessica said pointedly. "Liz, why in the world did you ever bring the two of them together? Didn't you realize what you were starting?"

"Bring them together?" Elizabeth repeated blankly. "Wait a minute, Jess. I didn't do anything. All I did was encourage Abbie to enter the humor competition and then give her a little moral support when she was getting started. She and Steve became friends on their own."

"Well, I can't bear it." Jessica groaned. "There's no way I can go to the game tomorrow night and watch them mooning over each other. It's just too disgusting. Cara's probably never going to forgive me as it is."

"Look," Elizabeth said, "has something worse

happened, or are you just upset because you think Abbie has a crush on Steve?"

"I happen to have proof," Jessica declared.

"Proof of what?"

"Proof that Abbie's the one who's been writing those letters to Steve." Jessica proceeded to explain how she had seen Abbie slipping one of the letters—on the same pink stationery as the others—into her bag right in front of her. "It's obvious. She's been writing Steve all along. I don't think she ever liked either of us. It was Steve she wanted. And now she's got him!"

Elizabeth looked stunned. "You really saw Abbie holding one of those letters?"

"I'm telling you, Liz, I did! She was obviously about to leave the letter for Steve, and she stopped when she saw me. Well, her letters are obviously doing the trick, too, because Steve seems too far gone for help."

Elizabeth frowned. "I can't believe Abbie would do something like this. I really trusted her. I was sure she wouldn't be so underhanded!"

"Well, Miss Underhanded seems to have stolen Steve from Cara right in front of us. I feel just awful about Cara. And not only that, I'm sure she's going to kill me," Jessica said tragically.

Elizabeth was getting increasingly angry. "I don't think we can let her get away with this,

Jess. We've got to talk to her. I don't know about you, but I really feel betrayed. I mean, I thought Abbie genuinely liked us. I thought she was coming over here all the time because she wanted to be with us, not because she wanted to steal Steven from Cara!"

"I think what we ought to do is confront her, right in front of Steve. Tell her we know she wrote those letters and we know why."

Elizabeth frowned. "Well, we don't want to embarrass her," she said reluctantly. "Can't we talk to her alone?"

"Liz," Jessica cried, "how can you be such a softie? This girl has been completely using us for the past few weeks, and you're worried about embarrassing her? After she's been sending love notes to Steve, knowing about Cara the whole time?"

"You've got a point," Elizabeth said grimly. She couldn't believe Abbie would do something so low. Jessica was right. The only thing to do was to storm inside and confront her face-to-face. If Steven still wanted to go out with her after learning how sneaky and vile she'd been, that was his problem!

Lila didn't usually get so involved in her friends' crises, but she just couldn't stand the way Cara had looked when she stormed out of the cafeteria earlier that day. She felt she had to do something to comfort her friend, even if all she could do to console her was tell her about all the times she herself had been treated wretchedly by guys. On her way home, Lila decided to stop at Cara's apartment and see if she was there. Lila hoped Cara had cooled off and hadn't rushed over to the Wakefields' after school.

Lila jumped out of her lime-green Triumph and hurried up the front walk of the apartment building. She rang the buzzer in the entryway and was relieved to hear Cara's voice.

"Oh, Cara, I'm so glad you're home. I came to commiserate with you."

Cara buzzed Lila in and opened her apartment door a few moments later. She looked incredibly forlorn. "I don't want to talk about it," she said unhappily. "I've already decided. I'm never going to mention Steven Wakefield's name again. That's it. I'm not going to confront him, and I'm not going to talk to him. I'm going to completely forget that he exists."

"Cara, be reasonable," Lila said, barging right in. "Have you got some iced tea or something? It's absolutely *boiling* out there. And you and I need to sit down and have a long talk. I can't stand seeing you look so sad, Cara! Steve isn't worth it. Think of all his bad qualities."

"Like what?" Cara demanded.

"Well . . . he doesn't have any money, for one thing," Lila said, opening the Walkers' refrigerator and frowning at the contents. "And he really hasn't treated you very well, if you ask me. I mean, where's the romance? No fancy restaurants, no long-stemmed red roses arriving unexpectedly at your door."

"I don't care about any of those things, Lila. I just want things to be the way they were before," Cara said, her eyes filling with tears.

"Before what? I don't understand what's changed," Lila said calmly. "Are you sure you aren't remembering things as being better than they ever were?"

"No, I'm positive. I know when things changed, too," Cara said miserably. "Remember when Jessica started giving me such a hard time about all the romance going out of our relationship, about taking each other for granted and all that? And then she suggested I ought to start acting aloof to add some mystery to the relationship."

"I remember. And that was good advice. I agree with Jessica."

"Well, it sure didn't work for me." Cara sighed. "I actually was dumb enough to believe it would, too. I started thinking things over and I got completely paranoid about Steve and me. I started thinking that he really was taking me for granted, that I'd been way too open with him, that our relationship was just too *easy*. Boy, was I ever stupid." She shook her head. "I decided to send Steven these anonymous love letters. I really went all out. I went and bought this romantic stationery, and I even put perfume on the paper. I wrote these schmaltzy letters and then sent them without signing them."

"That sounds like a good way to put some romance back in your relationship," Lila said, pouring herself some iced tea. "What happened? Didn't he like them?"

"The worst thing in the world is that I don't know *what* he thought of them. I tried to ask him about the first one, and he got incredibly defensive. He acted as if the letter was from someone else. So I got even more paranoid, thinking that he must like some girl at college or he wouldn't be acting that way."

"You've never told him the letters were from you?"

"No. The whole point was to be mysterious," Cara said miserably. "But instead of being mysterious in a good way, those stupid letters seemed to make us dishonest with each other. It was like we were both trying to find something out without asking. I was hurt and jealous over his reaction, but I never told him how I felt. I just acted weird and insecure."

Lila shook her head. "Well, that doesn't change the fact that Steve's been a real jerk. What about Abbie? Aren't you angry about that?"

Cara's eyes filled with tears. "I just feel rotten," she said softly. "After the way I've been behaving, I almost don't blame Steven for being interested in someone else."

"That," Lila said firmly, "is the dumbest thing I've ever heard. If I were you, I'd be so angry at Steve that I'd—I'd . . . well, I don't know what I'd do. Kill him, maybe."

Cara shook her head. "At first I was angry. Now I'm just sad," she said softly. "I feel that Steve and I have lost something incredibly precious, and I don't know how it happened."

"What if I told you that I'm pretty certain Abbie stole Steve right out from under you?" Lila demanded. "Wouldn't *that* make you mad?"

Cara shook her head. "I don't believe anyone can *steal* anyone else. This is Steve we're talking about, not some sort of material possession. The truth is, Steve and I have lost the ability to talk honestly to each other. Without that, there's no way our love can stay alive. That's all there is to it. What's happening with Abbie . . . well"

—Cara took a deep breath and shrugged her shoulders—"I can't pretend I like it. In fact, if I really think about it, it makes me feel so sick, I can't stand it. But I can't blame anything on anyone else. This is a problem between Steve and me."

"Well, if that's the case, why are you sitting around here and sulking? Why don't you go over to the Wakefields' house and tell Steve exactly how you feel?"

Cara stared unhappily at the ground. "It's too late, Lila. I'll never be able to talk to him now, not after all that's happened."

"Cara," Lila said, crossing her arms and eyeing her friend impatiently, "you get up right now. I'm going to drive you over to the Wakefields to talk to Steve, even if I have to *drag* you over there."

Cara didn't say anything for a minute. When she looked up again, her eyes were shining with tears. "OK," she said, "you're right. I should go. I guess I've just been putting this off because I'm afraid the next time I face Steve will be the last. But you're right. There's really no point in putting off the inevitable."

"Hi, Liz! I've been waiting for you," Abbie began when Elizabeth, followed by Jessica, marched purposefully into the living room, where Abbie and Steven were seated on the couch. When she saw the look on Elizabeth's face, Abbie's voice faltered. "Is something wrong? You look angry."

"I *am* angry," Elizabeth said, staring at her. It was hard to believe, looking at mild, even-tempered Abbie, that she could be so scheming. But Jessica had seen the letter in her hand. She had evidence!

"Abbie," Elizabeth began, "when I started inviting you over here, I really believed you wanted to be friends. How could you treat us all so deviously?"

"What—what do you mean?" Abbie cried, her face pale.

"You know what she means," Jessica snapped. "Writing those love letters to Steven. Hanging around here waiting for him all the time. Doing everything you could to sabotage his relationship with Cara."

"Writing . . . but I didn't write those letters!" Abbie cried. She turned to Steven, her lips trembling. "Tell them, Steven. I didn't write those letters!"

"That's not what the saleswoman at the Pen and Paper shop said," Jessica said, glaring at her. "We know you bought that pink statio-

130

nery, Abbie. Face it. There's no point in lying anymore."

"I can't believe you'd do something like this," Elizabeth said reproachfully. "I trusted you, Abbie. If I'd known all you wanted was to get closer to Steve . . ."

Now it was Steven's turn to get upset. "*You* wrote those letters?" he said accusingly, staring at Abbie with a look of dawning horror in his eyes. "Abbie, how could you? How could you possibly do something so rotten, when I thought I could trust you, when I thought you were my friend?"

Abbie stared at the three of them in total disbelief, her face white as a sheet. She grabbed onto the couch armrest for support, and Elizabeth could see how unsteady she was.

Elizabeth knew how frail Abbie's ego was, and suddenly she was afraid for Abbie.

Eleven

Abbie couldn't believe her ears. Everything that had happened in the past half-hour, since Jessica had walked in and seen her holding Steven's letter, felt to her like a nightmare. It didn't seem as if this could really be happening. To listen to Elizabeth accuse her of all these horrible things. . . . Abbie took a deep breath. She could hear the blood pounding in her ears, and for one awful moment she was afraid she was going to faint.

For as long as she could remember, this was what Abbie had dreaded more than anything else—that someone would accuse her of doing something terrible, of hurting someone deeply. She had always worked so hard at being nice, at being the girl voted "most friendly" or "easiest to get along with." To do something that would hurt someone else, well, that was completely alien to her generous personality. It always had been. Part of the reason she had always knocked herself out doing things for other people was that she depended on other people's images of her as nice. She was, deep down, so insecure that she couldn't believe she was a nice girl unless the people around her confirmed it.

Now her worst nightmare was coming true. Not only was she being accused, but she was being accused by Elizabeth and Jessica and Steven, the three people she had come to like and respect more than anyone else. Her friends. She felt she had fought so hard to be accepted and liked by them, and now they were turning on her. All of them. It was a sickening feeling, and she felt almost dizzy from the blow.

The strangest thing of all was that her immediate reaction was to feel guilty! Was it because she really *did* like Steven? But that was crazy, she admonished herself. She hadn't done anything wrong.

Abbie took a deep breath. What she intended to do was to walk out of the house without a word and never speak to any of them again. To her astonishment, though, she found herself speaking out in her own defense.

"Listen," she said in a low, clear voice, "I didn't write those letters. I don't know who did, and I don't know who gave you the idea that *I* did, but it's nuts."

Elizabeth and Jessica exchanged glances. "The girl in the stationery store told us someone came in who looked just like you and bought the last box of stationery like that," Jessica said, convinced by now that the saleswoman really *had* identified the girl as Abbie.

"Well, she's wrong. I would never do something like that. The truth is, I haven't done one single thing that I have any reason to be ashamed of." She looked directly at Steven when she spoke. "You know that, Steve. I'm surprised you could turn on me the way you did. I sat here and listened and listened while you told me how upset you were about Cara. And I never took advantage of your uncertainty. I encouraged you over and over again to talk things out with her, to try to make things work. How can you possibly think I was trying to sabotage your relationship with her?"

Steven was quiet for a minute. "I don't know what to think," he said. "If it's true you wrote those letters . . ."

Abbie felt something snap in her then. "I *didn't* write those letters, Steven! I can't believe this is happening! All my life I've tried to be nice and do things for other people," she said in a quiet voice. "Now, for the first time ever, I can see how crazy that was. I tried to get all of you to like me. I liked you, and I wanted to be your friend. But it's obvious that I went about things the wrong way. Not one of you trusts me. You think I was just using you. I see now what really comes of being nice to people."

Elizabeth stared down at the floor. Something in Abbie's voice pierced her deeply. She could tell how hurt Abbie was, and suddenly she was filled with empathy. Perhaps they *had* misjudged her.

"I'm going to leave now," Abbie said finally. "But I want all of you to know that I had nothing whatever to do with those letters. I haven't done anything underhanded or scheming since I walked into this house. It was just—" Her eyes filled with tears. "It was just that I liked you, all of you, and I wanted you to like me." She took a long, shuddering breath, and with her head held high, she turned and walked out of the room.

It was by far the hardest thing Abbie had ever done in her whole life. But the amazing thing was that through the pain she felt OK, really OK, for the first time in a long while.

She had stood up for herself. For the first time she could ever remember, she had defended herself. And what's more, she knew she was right. And that feeling made the pain, and even the loss of her new friends, worth it. For once she could honestly say she felt good about herself.

Cara was terrified to knock on the Wakefields' door. What a strange feeling, she thought. She had gone over there dozens and dozens of times, and she'd never thought twice about it.

Well, there was no point in delaying. What she needed was to face Steven, to tell him about the letters, and to decide with him what they should do next. She didn't even know whether or not she hoped that they could salvage things. She just knew that they needed to talk, honestly and openly.

"Cara!" Jessica exclaimed, opening the door after Cara knocked. "What—I mean, Steve didn't say that you—"

"I've come over to talk to him," Cara said simply. "Is he here?"

Jessica gulped. "Uh, yes. He's in the living room with Liz."

Cara nodded and, with a look of determination, crossed the foyer. This wasn't going to be easy, but it had to be done. "Steven?" she said, coming into the living room followed by Jessica.

Steven turned to her, a host of conflicting expressions crossing his handsome face as he stared at her.

"I need to talk to you," she said. She looked at Elizabeth. "Actually, I need to talk to you alone." Her glance fell on the sheet of pink stationery lying on the table, and she picked up the letter ruefully. "You got this, huh? Did you ever guess these letters were coming from me?"

Elizabeth gasped, and Jessica went pale. "From—from you?" Jessica stammered.

Steven stared at her. "Cara, why were you sending me anonymous letters? I thought—"

Cara sighed. "I was afraid we were beginning to take each other for granted. I wanted"—she glanced meaningfully at Jessica—"more mystery between us. I just wasn't prepared for the way you acted when you got the first one. You seemed so secretive about it. It made me really insecure."

Steven clapped his hand to his forehead. "I can't believe the letters were coming from *you*," he repeated. "Cara, that never occurred to me! And you know why I didn't tell you about them? Because—" He broke off, a troubled frown creasing his forehead. "Because they were written on the same stationery that Tricia used to use. I felt like I was seeing a ghost when I got the first letter."

Cara turned pale. "Oh, no," she gasped. "Steven, I can't believe that! I bought that stationery at the Pen and Paper shop. I asked the salesgirl for something romantic, and she suggested that paper. If I'd known . . ."

"There was no way you could have known," Steven said, getting up from the couch and approaching Cara. "I just can't believe I never had the guts to talk to you about it." He wrapped his arms around her and drew her close.

"Jessica," Elizabeth said softly, "something tells me this is a good time for us to get lost."

Jessica nodded. It was obvious that Cara and Steven had a lot to discuss and they wanted to be alone.

And Jessica and Elizabeth needed to put their heads together, too. Because it was equally clear to them that they had a major problem on their hands. What on earth were they going to say to Abbie Richardson?

* * *

"I just can't believe we weren't able to tell each other how we felt," Cara said, staring deeply into Steven's eyes.

"I can't, either. When I think of how convinced I was that you'd be furious and upset about those letters, that somehow you'd be jealous or blame me or something. . . ."

"We've really acted insane," Cara said, shaking her head. She and Steven had taken a walk together in order to get some privacy. No sooner were they outside than the truth began to pour forth.

"I felt so insecure," Cara confessed. "You seemed to be getting more and more distant from me, so I started to cling to you, hoping to keep you. I guess it backfired."

Steven nodded. "Yes, because I felt confused by how demanding and possessive you'd become. I just wanted to move away from you."

"The worst thing was that we stopped communicating," Cara said. "Steve, we can't ever let that happen to us again."

"I know," Steven said, stroking her shoulder. "It was awful. We won't let it happen again. But, Cara, sending me anonymous letters just doesn't seem like something you'd do."

Cara blushed. "Your sister had me convinced that there wasn't enough mystery in our relationship. I thought she was talking nonsense at first, but then when you came home, you were acting funny—kind of distant and not as loving as you usually are. I was worried, and I thought Jessica might actually have a point."

"I *was* acting distant," Steven agreed. "I guess it was a mixture of things, mostly the fact that I was feeling crummy. Between that and worrying about schoolwork, well"—he shook his head—"I guess I wasn't as warm and affectionate to you as I usually am. But I suppose I counted on the fact that if something was really wrong, you'd say something to me about it."

"But you did the same thing," Cara reminded him. "Instead of telling me what was bothering you, you kept it all to yourself. I had no idea what was going on. All I knew was that you and I were drifting further and further apart."

"Let's make each other a promise," Steven said, pulling her close. "Let's promise that no matter what, from now on we're going to be completely open with each other. No secrets, no mysteriousness. If something's wrong, and it will be sometimes, because we live apart and we're both strong-minded people, we'll tell each other right away. And we'll work as hard as we can to make things better."

Cara nodded solemnly. "Well, if we're going

to be totally honest with each other, I have to ask you about Abbie. Lila told me that you asked her to the basketball game tomorrow night." Her voice cracked as she felt tears rising to the surface. "Do you . . . what's going on there? Tell me how you feel about her."

"Oh, no. Abbie," Steven said, looking stricken. When Cara's eyes widened with alarm, he hugged her reassuringly. "Don't be a dope," he admonished her. "I happen to be in love with *you*, remember? Abbie is a friend. She's given me some great advice, advice I really should've taken. The reason I just looked so upset is that I was remembering what we did to her—Liz and Jessica and I. We all accused her of being the one to write those letters. We accused her of trying to steal me away from you."

Cara's eyes widened. "You did?"

Steven nodded. "The worst thing was that it was actually the exact opposite. I started confiding in Abbie when I felt as though you and I couldn't talk openly, but from the beginning she encouraged me to come to you and explain— about the letters, about everything." Steven was miserable. "Poor Abbie, I can't believe we did that to her!"

"I can't either," Cara said in a soft whisper. Hard as it was to imagine, she was actually

142

empathizing with Abbie now. And she wanted to do whatever she could to help the girl. She felt she owed Abbie a few apologies herself— for not inviting her to her party, for one thing.

The question was, would Abbie even be willing to listen to their explanations, or would she tell them she never wanted to talk to them as long as she lived?

"I don't see why I have to be the one to call her," Jessica muttered.

"You're the one who accused her!" Elizabeth cried. "I mean, we *all* accused her. But you're the one who insisted you'd seen her clutching one of those letters. Go on, Jess. Just dial her number."

The twins were gathered with Steven and Cara in the kitchen, staring at the wall phone. The prospect of calling Abbie was so awful that none of them could bring themselves to do it. Elizabeth couldn't stop berating herself.

"Every time I think about Abbie, I want to cry! She's been so kind and generous to us all. So trusting, so sweet—and what do we do? Turn around and stab her in the back."

"Yeah," Jessica said miserably. "And the worst thing is, she's such a—well, you know, such a pushover. She'll probably try to jump out a window or something. She's got such low self-esteem that our accusations probably made her despise herself even more."

"Wait a minute," Steven said reflectively. "Abbie didn't slink out of here looking guilty. She stood up for herself, remember? Actually, she behaved with a lot more dignity than any of us. Maybe she doesn't have such low self-esteem after all."

"I'm going to call her," Cara said suddenly, picking up the phone receiver. "I have an apology I want to make to her myself. Let's see if she'll let us all come over to her house."

With a look of determination Cara began to dial.

Twelve

Abbie was sitting on the front porch waiting for them when the two cars pulled up in her driveway twenty minutes later. She was nervous, but she didn't look it. She held her head high and looked straight at the three Wakefields and Cara as they approached her. Never again, she thought, would she act in a way that would let people push her around. From now on she was going to be strong, she was going to stick up for herself.

"Abbie," Cara said, "we all owe you an apology. But let me start by saying I did something really stupid. Well, actually, I did a lot of stupid things. But one thing I learned this week is that keeping quiet isn't the way to solve problems. I told you about my party,

145

and then I found out that I could only have a certain number of guests. I tried to pretend that keeping quiet would make the problem go away. Instead, all I did was hurt you. I'm really sorry."

Abbie regarded Cara. "Thank you for explaining," she said carefully. "My feelings *were* hurt."

The twins exchanged glances, but suddenly the planned-out speech Elizabeth had intended to make seemed all wrong to her, and she ran forward and flung her arms around Abbie's neck. "We were such a bunch of jerks!" she cried. "Do you think you can ever forgive us?"

Abbie's perfect composure began to falter. Her lower lip trembled, and her eyes filled with tears. "I like you all so much," she said painfully. "But I can't let you stand around and accuse me of something I never did. I know I wasn't wrong, and that's all there is to it."

"*You* weren't wrong. *We* were," Jessica said. "Abbie, please forgive us. We're really sorry, all three of us."

Abbie looked at them and for the first time warmth flickered in her blue eyes. "Well," she said, relenting a little, "I guess I ought to thank you as much as accept your apology. You guys taught me a lesson this afternoon that I'll never forget."

"What's that?" Steven asked her.

"I've always been so down on myself," Abbie replied. "My natural inclination is to take the blame, to volunteer to do the dirty work, to make people treat me like a doormat. You guys forced me to do something I've never done before. You forced me to stick up for myself. And that's more important to me than anything else."

"You're right, Abbie. You did stick up for yourself. And you made us realize what real friendship is," Elizabeth said quietly. "We did something inexcusable this afternoon. We blamed you for something without having evidence."

"So who *did* write those letters?" Abbie asked, perplexed.

Cara hung her head. "I did," she said in a low voice. "You're not the only one who has an insecurity problem, Abbie. I was trying to add some excitement to my romance with Steve. Instead, I almost wrecked it."

Abbie appeared startled for a moment, but when the information sank in, she smiled and said, "Why don't we all go inside and make some lemonade or something?"

Steven let out a long breath. "Does that mean you don't hate us? You're willing to forgive us for acting like such jerks?"

Abbie smiled again and looked at each of them in turn. "Of course I forgive you," she said simply. "Isn't that what friendship's all about?"

"Just promise me one more thing," Steven said. "I invited you to the game tomorrow, and I'm not going to go back on my word." He looked from Abbie to Cara. "If my dad can get another ticket for the game, can we all go together?"

Cara and Abbie looked at each other for a moment. Then both girls burst out laughing. "Why not?" they said in unison. Everyone joined in their laughter as the tension among them turned into amusement. Abbie and Elizabeth linked arms as they turned to go inside, and Abbie's face was positively radiant.

For the first time she could remember, Abbie thought, she had *real* friends beside her. And she had learned, the hard way, what friendship was really about. For once, she felt like an equal among her friends, and she knew this was a lesson she would never, ever forget for as long as she lived. She had learned to stand up for herself, and that was the most important lesson of all.

Cara covered her ears as Steven let out an enthusiastic shout. The Wakefields—plus Cara and Abbie—were at the basketball game. The Lakers were ahead, and Steven was too much of a fan not to show his appreciation. "This is fun," Cara said to Abbie, giving her a friendly pat on the arm. "I'm really glad Mr. Wakefield got an extra ticket so all of us could come."

Abbie nodded, her eyes shining. She had never been to a professional basketball game before, and the truth was, she was having a wonderful time. So much had changed since the big showdown with Elizabeth and Jessica the day before! In fact, Abbie could hardly believe it when she looked back on the events of the last twenty-four hours.

First, and most important, she had won *The Oracle* competition! "Jenny" was going to be a weekly feature in the school paper. Abbie had almost fainted when Mr. Collins had called her at home on Saturday. It would be officially announced in the paper the following week, and her first entry would also appear. "Yours was by far the best entry," he had said, shaking her hand. "Welcome aboard, Abbie. It's going to be a treat working with you."

Abbie couldn't believe her ears. "You mean I won? I really won, fair and square?" She had thought back on all the hours she put in helping out Amy Sutton with her column. And her cartoon had *still* won! She had been so excited that she couldn't wait to get home and tell her parents. It was the first time Abbie could remember having something that was hers—completely and entirely hers. She intended to do a terrific job on the strip.

When Elizabeth had told her that her father had been able to get one more ticket and that the Wakefields still wanted to go to the Lakers game, as planned, Abbie felt funny at first. She didn't know whether or not she would feel comfortable spending time with Cara and Steven together. But now, listening to the cheering crowd, she was glad she had come. It was clear that everything between Steven and Cara was terrific again, and, actually, Abbie didn't feel the least bit awkward about it. She was just happy to be there, having a good time with people she knew liked her and trusted her, people who were her friends.

Mr. and Mrs. Wakefield pulled the twins aside during halftime when Steven, Abbie, and Cara went down to the concession stand for some pretzels and soft drinks. "Girls, we've got some big news for you," Alice Wakefield said with a twinkle in her blue eyes. "We wanted to tell you earlier, but there hasn't been time. Steve doesn't know yet. This is a total surprise."

The twins exchanged glances. "What? Tell us!" Jessica shrieked.

"I got a letter last week from your Aunt Laura," Mrs. Wakefield continued, "but I didn't want to say anything until we were a hundred percent certain that it was going to come through."

"Aunt Laura!" the twins cried. Laura, their mother's sister, lived in Tucson, Arizona. She was one of the twins' favorite relatives, and they loved hearing news about her, and about her daughter, Kelly, the twins' first cousin, who was the same age they were. Jessica and Elizabeth hadn't seen her in ages.

"How's Kelly?" Jessica asked. "Are we going to get to visit her soon?"

Ned Wakefield laughed. "As a matter of fact, you are. But the mountain is coming to Muhammad, as the old saying goes."

"What?" Elizabeth said, puzzled.

"Your father means that Kelly is coming here." Mrs. Wakefield smiled. "How does that sound to you?"

The twins jumped up and down and hugged each other. They both adored Kelly, and the thought of a visit was wonderful. "I want her to stay in my room!" Jessica cried.

"That'll drive her right back to Arizona," Elizabeth said dryly. "No, let her stay in *my* room!"

"Girls," Mrs. Wakefield said, shaking her head, "she's going to be staying a little longer than you may think. I have a feeling that Steve's room will be best, as he'll be back at school when she arrives."

"Is she coming for a long time? Where's Aunt Laura going to be?" Jessica asked.

"That's the other big news. Aunt Laura is getting married. She's met a wonderful man— a widowed doctor who has two sons." Mrs. Wakefield sighed. "But Kelly isn't taking it very well. You know how much she idolizes her father. She can't stand the thought of anyone trying to replace him. Your aunt is hoping that if Kelly spends some time with us, she'll cool off a little and be more accepting of her new stepfather.''

Elizabeth was intrigued. Kelly had always fascinated her, and here would be a chance to get to know her pretty cousin better. Elizabeth only knew the barest facts about her aunt's divorce from her Uncle Greg. She knew that her uncle had left when Kelly was very little—only eight or nine years old. But it was true that Kelly adored her father, and Aunt Laura never stopped her when she insisted that he was the world's greatest dad.

It would be wonderful to see Kelly again, but Elizabeth sensed it might not be so wonderful for Kelly. Not with her mother planning to get remarried and a new father trying to step in between her and her real dad. Plus she would suddenly have to live with two stepbrothers.

She and Jessica would just have to do everything in their power to make their cousin feel welcome. Elizabeth could hardly wait to see her. She just hoped that she and Jessica would be able to help Kelly through the rocky time ahead.

Will Kelly's stay in Sweet Valley help her accept the situation at home? Find out in Sweet Valley High # 45, FAMILY SECRETS.

Get Ready for a Thrilling Time in Sweet Valley®!

☐ **26905 DOUBLE JEOPARDY #1**   **$2.95**

When the twins get part-time jobs on the Sweet Valley newspaper, they're in for some chilling turn of events. The "scoops" Jessica invents to impress a college reporter turn into the real thing when she witnesses an actual crime—but now no one will believe her! The criminal has seen her car, and now he's going after Elizabeth ... the twins have faced danger and adventure before ... but never like this!

Watch for the second Sweet Valley Thriller Coming in May

Prices and availability subject to change without notice.